In loving memory of Paul Alan Fahey

To Krystal—
thank you for
the work you do!
Be your Warrior
self always!
Katie

TOKEN OF CHOICE

By

Kathy Barron

CHAPTER ONE

The danger all started when Abigail and I went for a hike near Jemez Springs, New Mexico for our annual end of summer hike. We stuffed our backpacks with food and water and started out on the trailhead early morning while it was still cool.

Clear blue skies and the sweet, vanilla aroma of the ponderosa pines were intoxicating. We kept conversation to a minimum as we trekked up each switchback on the trail. The forest was abuzz with chattering birds and the scuffing of our boots on the dirt floor. My lungs thanked me with each deep breath of fresh, crisp mountain air. We were excited to get to the waterfall and have our yearly dip in the fresh water pool. This was a ritual of sorts for us.

Abigail and I had known each other for over ten years; first as friends and then as business partners. We met on a hiking trip with mutual friends on this same trail. She stood behind me when I twisted my ankle, basically carrying me down the remainder of the trail. We became fast friends and stayed in touch over the years taking vacations together. This hike became a yearly tradition.

Those ten years went by quickly. Buying the bar on a whim was the best decision I'd made in my life. It continued to be a successful venture and the people I have met along the way have been amazing. I could honestly say that my life had been great. So why did I feel like something was missing? A nagging feeling that there is more to life than what I see in front of me. Is it just the change in seasons?

We were the only ones on the trail and by the time we got to the waterfall, people were heading back down to the trailhead. There's nothing like being in the middle of the forest with only one other person. Just us and Mother Nature.

After a couple of hours of grazing, swimming and soaking in the sunrays, we grabbed our backpacks and headed back down the trail. The sun was descending, casting golden light through the trees. As we came around one of the last switchbacks overlooking the mountain ridge, my walking stick landed on a dark, flat stone. I squatted down, picked up the stone and turned it over in my palm. Staring up at me was a fossil the size of a half dollar.

"Hey Abigail, wait up," I yelled as I stood up, admiring my treasure. "I found something."

"What is it?" Abigail asked as she turned around and walked towards me. I stretched out my hand and showed her the fossil.

"The fossil looks like the scales of a fish. I've never seen anything like this before," I said, looking at the ground to see if there were any more stones like it.

"That's cool," she said with child-like excitement as she took it out of my hand.

The stone slipped out of her fingers. In slow motion, I reached out to catch it and my foot slipped off the edge of the trail. My hands frantically clawed at the dirt and rocks in an attempt to stop my fall. As I slid down the side of the mountain on my stomach something abruptly stopped me. My heart pounded in my ears and I couldn't catch my breath.

A man with dark brown hair, weathered face and deep brown eyes was sitting on a boulder next to me. I looked down at my foot and his hand was gripping my foot. Where did he come from? He smiled as he placed my foot on top of a tree root.

"Are you okay?" Looking upward toward the ledge, I saw Abigail peering over at me.

"Yeah." I spit out dirt.

I looked over my shoulder to thank the mysterious man, but he was gone. Did I imagine him? The shock of the fall must have made me hallucinate.

"Here. Grab my hand," Abigail said, reaching down toward me.

She pulled me back up on the trail. Still on my stomach, I peered over the edge. I couldn't have imagined him; his grip was strong under my foot, his cologne still tingled my nostrils with its musky, calming scent. Sighing, I sat up and did a quick inventory of my legs and arms.

"Are you sure you're okay?" Abigail asked, kneeling next to me.

"I'm a bit shaken. A little scraped up and dirty. So you ended up catching the stone, huh?" I said, pointing to her hand.

"Yeah. Still have good reflexes." She opened her hand and I took the stone from her dirty, sweaty palm.

After a few minutes of regrouping, we grabbed our packs and started down the trail. A couple of hours later the parking lot came into view. My body was sore and my heart beat through my sweat-soaked shirt but I had survived. As I opened my water bottle, I poured the remains on top of my head to cool off. Abigail popped open the trunk of her car and we tossed our packs inside.

As we drove through the small town of Jemez, my mouth grew dry and my chest tightened. I took a few deep breaths in hopes of calming myself down, but the feeling only intensified as we traveled along the road.

"Can we pull over for a sec?" I groped for the door handle.

"Are you alright?" Abigail said looking at me with a furrowed brow.

I threw open the door as soon as the car stopped and walked unsteadily to the back. The trunk popped open, and I rummaged through the pack for a water bottle. I sat on the edge of the trunk, gulped some water and took a deep breath. Looking up toward the mountainside, the man from the cliff was a few feet from the car. He was perched on a large rock with arms crossed against his chest.

"What the..." I said under my breath, almost falling inside the trunk. "Who is this guy and how is he always where I am?"

"How's it going back there?" Abigail shouted out her window.

"Just getting some water." I turned in her direction and looked back to look at the man, but he disappeared. I scanned the side of the mountain with no luck; he was gone.

"I need to get my eyes checked," I said, took another drink of water and slammed the trunk closed.

As we came around a bend in the road, cars were stopped up ahead. Abigail quickly slowed down and came to a complete stop behind a few cars.

I poked my head out of the window to see if there was anything happening up ahead. "Oh my god! There's a car hanging off the cliff."

Abigail gasped and peered over the other cars in front of us.

I unbuckled my seat belt and leaned out of the window. "Someone is running toward the car."

I jumped out and jogged toward the car hanging off the ledge. The driver in the car in front of us looked more annoyed than concerned, so I kept moving toward the accident. A man stood by the driver's side door. With my heart picking up speed, I walked up to the passenger side of the car. The windshield above the steering wheel was smashed with blood smeared on it. The woman slumped, unconscious, her head leaning to one side and her black hair was matted down with blood.

As I stepped back from the car, I saw the two front wheels hanging precariously off the ledge. My vision narrowed and in my head I heard my mom screaming.

I could see myself standing outside my parent's station wagon, watching my dad struggling to get his legs free from under the steering wheel. My mom was yelling at him to hurry. He pulled on his legs and pounded his fists on the wheel. He tried to move his body but it wouldn't budge. My mom grabbed my arm and was saying something to me but I couldn't make out the words. As she turned back to my dad, the car inched forward to the edge of the cliff. A man was shouting and a car horn honked.

I looked over at the man standing by the driver's side door.

"How are we going to get her out?" He yelled.

My t-shirt was soaked with sweat and my heart raced. I looked at him with a blank stare and shrugged my shoulders.

I reached down to gently pull open the passenger door. Even with this slight move, the car creaked forward. I stopped, holding my breath. The guy raised his hands in the air as if to say 'I give up' and stepped back from the car.

I slowly removed my hand from the handle and backed away. Sweat was dripping down my face. I needed a moment to regroup.

Just then, the woman moaned. I rushed over to the driver side and peered inside.

"What happened?" she said, turning toward me dazed.

"You're gonna be okay," I said in the calmest voice I could conjure up. She reached for the steering wheel.

"Wait. Don't move." I gently reached out to her.

She stopped mid reach and looked at me with wide eyes.

"Just stay where you are and we will get you out. But please try not to move."

She looked straight ahead. "Why is there blood on the windshield?" she asked touching her forehead. "Oh my

God! I'm bleeding!" She screamed, staring at the blood on her hand.

"You hit your head on the windshield. You're going to be okay. My name is Kristy. What's your name?"

"Um... it's... it's... Carol." Bloody tears ran down her face.

"Carol, we're going to get you out of here." *Keep it together, Kristy. You need to keep it together. You can do this.* An image of my dad's face flashed in my mind.

I stepped back from the car, wiped my face with my hands and looked over at the guy. "What's your name?" I asked him.

"David," he said, looking pale and wide eyed.

"Okay, David, we need to pull Carol out by using the passenger side door. Her door is too smashed and won't open," I said with as much confidence as I could muster.

"We'll have her unbuckle the seatbelt, and as she's doing that, I'll open the passenger side door."

David nodded, wiping his hand across his forehead.

"Once I have the door open, it's crucial we grab her and get her out of the car as fast as possible. Do you understand?" I asked, taking hold of his shoulder gently.

He jerked his head as if nodding.

"Okay, Carol?" I said, leaning into the driver side window. She looked straight ahead and didn't move.

"David and I are going to walk around to the passenger side of the car. When I tell you to, unbuckle your seatbelt and s-l-o-w-l-y turn your back to us. Do you understand?"

"Yes. I understand," Carol mumbled with tears streaming down her face.

I motioned David to follow me as I walked around the back of the car to the passenger side door.

"I'll need you here with me so we can pull her out together. It needs to happen in one fell swoop. No hesitation, no second guessing. On my go, we'll grab her and pull her out. Got it?"

"Got it," David muttered. We took our positions.

"Okay, Carol. Unbuckle your seatbelt now," I said, reaching down to the door handle.

I held my breath as she unbuckled the seatbelt. The front of the car jostled forward, creaking and groaning. My breath caught in my throat as I tried not to show my terror. I opened the door quickly as soon as the seatbelt slid off Carol. Grabbing her underneath her shoulders, I pulled as hard as I could without hurting her. I felt David come in beside me and grab Carol's waist.

The hood of the car started to tilt downward with an ominous slow screech. But Carol won't budge. I looked over to see her right leg stuck under the steering wheel. *Oh no you don't. This is not going to happen.*

"Pull harder," I yelled at David.

He grunted and Carol screamed in agony. The car started to slide toward the river below, but we gave Carol one last yank, and her feet cleared the car door just as it went over the ledge.

David and I were flung backward on the ground with Carol on top of us. My ears filled with the sound of metal grinding down the side of the rocky cliff, followed by a loud crash.

"Kristy? Are you okay?" Abigail said from above me.

I looked up at her but all I could do is let my head drop to the ground and close my eyes.

CHAPTER TWO

"I'm exhausted and wound up at the same time," I said to Abigail as we walked into my apartment. I tossed my backpack by the front door and walked to the kitchen. "You want a beer? I need something to calm my nerves."

"Sure, I'll take one."

"What a day." Abigail plopped down on the couch.

"No kidding. Never in my wildest dreams did I think I would fall down a hillside and rescue a woman from an accident today." I sat on the edge of the solid oak coffee table. "I'm glad she'll be okay."

"You doing okay?" Abigail said reaching for the beer.

"What do you mean?"

"You know, with your dad's accident? I can only imagine how today affected you emotionally."

"Yeah, I'm okay. In a way it was a kind of redemption for not being able to save my dad." I take a long drink from the beer bottle.

As I set the beer on my thigh, it hit a hard object. I pulled the stone out of my pocket. "I forgot about this." I smoothed it over with my thumb.

Abigail took it from me and held it in the air between her thumb and forefinger.

"I wonder if it has magic powers," she snickered, giving me a sideways look. "Be careful, you might wake up tomorrow with a super power of getting all the women you desire. Oh wait, you already have that power."

I laughed out loud.

"Seriously, though, I bet Paige would love to see this fossil since she's the real expert on rocks and things." Abigail tossed me the stone.

"That's right. I forgot she collects this stuff." I caught the stone in my right hand and shoved it back into my pocket.

"Well, as much as I would like to sit and chat, I need to get going. I'm beat." Abigail placed her beer bottle on the table and we both stood up.

"Thanks for the great hike, Kristy." Abigail reached out and hugged me. As she released her embrace, she leaned in and kissed me on the lips.

"What are you doing?" I asked moving my head back.

"I'm sorry. I don't know what came over me." Abigail stepped back. Her face was flush.

"We're just friends, Abigail. We've had this talk already, remember?" I said moving my hands like an umpire would call a baseball player safe at the plate.

"You're right. I'm sorry. Guess I got caught up in today's emotional rollercoaster. It will never happen again." Abigail rushed out of the apartment leaving me standing with my mouth agape.

What a weird way to end the day.

I cleaned up the beer bottles and dragged my aching and tired body to the bedroom, switched on the light and went over to the window. Reaching up to close the drapes, I caught sight of a woman with long flowing black hair standing across from me in the shadows of the streetlight. She wore a dark cape that reached her ankles and a collar up high against her neck. Her glowing hazel eyes scanned me briefly and then she slowly walked down the street and turned the corner.

I smacked my forehead into the glass window as my eyes followed her.

"Ow. Smart move, dipshit," I said, rubbing my head.

Pulling the drapes together, I was unable to shake the sight of the woman's cold glowing eyes watching me.

Walking over to the bed, I took the stone out of my pocket and placed it on the nightstand. A rainbow of colors glistened from the fossil under the lamplight. I crawled into bed, falling asleep as soon as my head hit the pillow.

I'm standing in the middle of the desert with golden red rocks towering over me, like I'm in some kind of canyon. Ankle deep water swirled around my feet. I lifted my right foot to see if the water was real, and it dripped off my foot, making ripples below. My fingers brushed the water's surface and, as I lifted my hand, a large shadow appeared over me. I looked up to see a tall Native American man with long brown hair. Two thin braids framed his tan face and multiple shell necklaces hung from his neck, cascading down his chest.

"W—who are you?" I said, reaching for something to lean up against but all I feel is air.

The man stared directly at me with gentle brown eyes. He put his right hand over his heart and bowed his head.

Not sure what the gesture meant, I continued to stare at him, open-mouthed and eyes wide. The man said nothing, took his hand off his heart and motioned me to come closer. I slowly inched my way forward, not taking my eyes off of him. He placed his open palm on my heart as I reached his outstretched hand. Our eyes locked and electricity coursed through my body. Feeling lightheaded, my legs gave out and everything went dark.

CHAPTER THREE

Although it was 11am, I still lay in bed staring into space. I kept telling myself to get up and start my day, but the energy I needed to put my feet on the floor was sapped by my thoughts. The events of yesterday ran on a loop like a movie in my mind. The woman standing outside my window and the dream were really messing with my head.

I rolled over onto my stomach and burrowed my head under the pillow. Unable to muffle the constant chatter in my head, I threw off the covers. As I got out of bed, I glanced over at the stone on the nightstand and got ready for work.

The Broken Chalice was a lesbian dance club and bar I co-owned with Abigail. This was our fifth year of business. We met Randi on one of our annual vacations to Santa Fe. The owner was looking to sell the bar and we were hungry for business venture. So far it had been a great success. It helped to be the only lesbian bar located downtown on the outskirts of the Plaza.

"Kristy! What are you doing here?" Randi, one of the bartenders asked, when I arrived.

"Hey Randi, just here to help out." I smiled as I walked past her.

Walking into the office, I found Paige sitting at her desk staring at the computer screen.

"Hey Paige. I wanted to show you a stone I found while hiking yesterday." I pulled it from my pocket and held it up for her to see.

"That is cool," Paige exclaimed.

Paige joined the Broken Chalice team a few years ago after we met her at a gem show Abigail dragged me to at the convention center. Paige saw me wandering by her booth and pulled me in with her charm. She showed me some crystals and shared way more information than I wanted to know about stones. She was unemployed and helping a friend for the day. We exchanged contact information and after a month of talking, I offered her the bookkeeper position. After all this time, I finally had something unusual to show her.

"Where did you get this?" She took the stone and turned it over in her palm.

"Abigail and I were hiking up by Jemez Springs. Do you know what it is?"

"Well it's definitely a fossil of some kind. Can I take a photo of it so I can look it up when I get home?" Paige reached into her back pocket.

"Sure," I said, holding it in my palm.

Paige pointed the phone at the stone and the flash went off. "Hm. That's interesting. Let me take another photo." The camera flashed again. "That's really weird," she said, looking at the photo again.

"What's weird?" I asked, peeking over the phone.

"I can't see the pictures. Let me take a picture of you to see if it comes out."

"How about we take a picture of both of us?" I suggested, putting my arm around her shoulders.

Paige lifted up the phone and took the picture.

"Did it come out?" I asked, reaching for the phone.

"Um. I don't know if you want to see this, Kristy," Paige said not taking her eyes off of the phone.

"Of course I want to see it!" I said, grabbing it from her.

"What the…? What's this golden glow around me? Your phone is messed up." I shoved it back in her hand.

"I have no idea why that happened," Paige said, scrolling through the photos.

"Well, let me know if you figure it out. I need to get up front and help Randi. Talk to you later," I said, jogging down the hallway toward the bar.

Late in the night the women were bumping and grinding to DJ Rae's dance mixes. Randi looked over at me, wiping her forehead with a towel.

I smiled and turned to a gorgeous brunette at the bar. "What can I get you?"

"Just your phone number, Sweetie," she replied, smirking.

"I don't like to mix business with pleasure." I smiled.

"That's too bad. You're definitely missing out." She winked. "I guess I'll take a gin and tonic as a booby prize."

"I'll make sure this is the best booby prize you've ever gotten."

I put the drink on a napkin and slid it toward her. "It's on the house. Have a great time tonight." She lifted up the glass as if to toast the occasion, smiled and disappeared into the crowd.

Rinsing some glasses in the sink, I got the sense I was being watched. I lifted my head slightly but didn't see anyone. Quickly putting the glasses into the dishwasher, I looked up again and found a woman standing at the bar who wasn't there a moment ago. A large, round, translucent emerald green crystal hung from her neck, slightly covered by her long blond hair. The stiff collar of her long, dark coat hid the sides of her face. Her mesmerizing stone blue eyes stared back at me.

No, *through* me.

For a split second, the music faded to the background, the women surrounding the bar were blurry and all action seemed in slow motion. A strange calm settled in my chest and my breathing was barely noticeable. The spell was broken by the sound of glass crashing from Randi's side of the bar.

My face felt hot. I put my hands on the bar to lean in closer. "How can I help you?"

"It's more like how can I help you," her hot breath said in my ear.

I pointed to myself, eyebrows raised.

She leans in closer. "I came to warn you about the stone."

How did she know about the stone? Not able to speak, her hand slipped over mine. "It's a dark power, Kristy. It's not for the faint of heart."

I froze in place by her touch.

"How do you know my name?" I asked, sliding my hand out from hers. "How do you know about the stone?"

"Heed my warning. It will bring chaos into your life and those around you." She played with the crystal dangling from her neck and the light shined in my eyes blindingly. I turned my head and held up my hand to protect my face.

I pulled my hand away and she was no longer standing at the bar. I frantically scanned the dance floor, but the sea of people swallowed her up.

I looked over at Randi to see if she noticed what just happened, but she's too busy flirting with the women dancing. Suddenly, I felt light headed. I motioned to Randi that I needed to take a break. I closed the office door and leaned up against it for a minute to catch my breath, and then collapsed onto the couch.

Taking a few deep breaths, I wiped the sweat off my face with both hands, slowly calming down. I replayed the conversation in my mind. How did she know I have the stone? What did she mean about chaos coming into my life?

After a few minutes, I sat up on the couch and felt the stone in my pocket. I took it out and stared it.

"Are you causing strange things to happen?"

An image of a dragonfly suddenly appeared on the face of the stone. Tilting it to one side, another faint image showed up. It's a hologram of a police shield. Oh my god.

This was the first time the stone had shown me images. My heart raced and my breath caught in my throat. I tightened my grip around the stone as my vision narrowed.

The stress from yesterday must have been finally taking its toll on me. Maybe this was what post-traumatic stress looked like. Having weird dreams, strange women knowing my name and people stalking me at night. Maybe I just needed to get away for a few days to forget about everything.

After splashing water on my face, I walked back out to the bar. It was just about closing time so the crowd had thinned out. Randi was cleaning up the bar while the last song played. I made sure everyone left the bar and locked the front door.

The night air was crisp and the scent of autumn permeated my nose. As I walked to my apartment, I paused at the railing overlooking the courtyard and tilted my head back. I took a deep breath and gazed at the star filled sky. It was in these moments that I realized just how small I was in this vast universe.

When I reached my apartment the door was slightly open. My heart raced, pounding in my ears. I slowly pushed open the door. Sliding my hand across the wall, I flipped the light switch up.

"What the...?" I gasped.

It looked like a tornado went through my apartment. The couch pillows were on the floor and sliced opened. Books were strewn all over the living room. Drawers had been pulled out of the armoire and things were scattered everywhere. I ran into my bedroom and the mattress was up on its side, the bedside table drawers dumped on the floor along with my clothes.

Frantic, I grabbed my phone and dialed Abigail's number.

"Hello," she said half asleep.

"Abigail. Someone broke into my apartment," I yelled into the phone.

"What? What are you talking about?" Abigail asked groggily.

"Someone has broken into my place. Get over here quick."

"Okay. Okay. I'll be right over."

I hung up and collapsed onto the box spring.

CHAPTER FOUR

"Oh my god. Are you okay?" Abigail said as she rushed down the hallway toward me.

Not able to hold it in any longer, I burst into tears. Abigail kneeled and hugged me.

"It's gonna be okay. I'm just glad you're not hurt." She hugged me tighter.

"Who would do this?" I said in between sobs.

"I don't know but we need to call the police." Abigail wiped tears from my cheeks. "Is anything missing?"

I looked at her wide-eyed. "I didn't even think of that." My eyes darted around the room taking a quick inventory. I rushed into the living room. "I can't even tell with everything scattered."

I stepped over flayed books, tossed drawers and gutted couch cushions. An elephant figurine without a trunk is lying on its side. Does that mean I'll have twenty years of bad luck?

"We need to call the police, Kristy." Abigail startled me out of my haze.

"Yeah, I guess." Tears burned my eyes and I squatted down to tend to the elephant.

A half hour later, two officers walked in accompanied by the squeaking and shuffling noises of their belts and shoes. The first one who introduced himself as Officer Stevens mulled around the living room with his hands on his gun belt pretending to be interested. The other officer, Sgt. Alvarez, asked if I have any enemies or business partners that would want to do this sort of thing.

"Well, she's my business partner." I pointed to Abigail. "So it couldn't be her." She gave a short wave to the sergeant.

"What type of business?" Sgt. Alvarez asked.

Abigail stepped toward the officer. "We own the Broken Chalice downtown. I'm Abigail, co-owner." She extended her hand and Sgt. Alvarez took it firmly.

"Ah." Sgt. Alvarez tilted her ear toward the squawking radio. "We'll have a technician come out to get some fingerprints." She nodded to the wandering officer who then mumbled something in his radio. "It shouldn't take them long to get here."

Sgt. Alvarez walked toward the bedroom, peeked into the kitchen and bathroom. "Does anyone have a key to your apartment? Employee, friend, family?"

"Um. I don't think so." I looked toward Abigail who shrugged her shoulders.

After what seemed like an eternity, there was another knock. Officer Stevens let in the technician. She put down a large black suitcase and flipped up the silver latches. Rubber gloves, brushes, tweezers and clear glass vials were neatly tucked between foam dividers. Without hesitating, she pulled on gloves, took out a brush and a black canister and walked to the door sprinkling black dust on the handle.

"I'll need the names of the people that have been to this apartment," The tech said as the brush danced over the door handle.

"Okay," I said with my hands in my pockets.

"I can take those names now, if you're ready." Sgt. Alvarez approached me with her notepad.

"The only people would be me and Abigail." I looked over at Abigail for some validation.

She scribbled in her notepad. "Anyone else you can think of?"

"No. I think that's it."

She closed the notepad and shoved it and the pen in her left breast pocket. The technician came into the living room, packed up her suitcase and snapped it shut. I jumped at the sound of metal against metal.

"You okay?" Sgt. Alvarez said, touching my arm.

"Yeah." What looked like the tail of a bug appeared just below her shirtsleeve. Interesting. Are cops allowed to have tattoos on their arms?

"What's your tattoo?" I asked pointing to her arm.

Sgt. Alvarez pulled up her shirtsleeve. "Oh, this old thing. It's a dragonfly. It reminds me to persevere and stay strong."

My heart skipped a beat. It's the same image that the stone showed me. Why would it show me a tattoo on a police...wait. The other image was a shield. I glanced up at the one pinned above her shirt pocket. Blood drained out of my face and my stomach dropped. My legs buckled under me and I was light headed.

"Are you sure you're okay?" Those words coming from Sgt. Alvarez sounded like they were coming out of a long tube. She reached for me.

"Maybe I need to sit down." She guided me over to the cushion less couch and I slowly sat down on the edge.

"Can you keep an eye on her?" She asked Abigail.

Abigail sat on the coffee table across from me and placed her hands on my knees. "You don't look so good."

"A bit on edge, I guess." I held my head in my hands.

"I got some partials and full prints. I should have the results in a few days." The technician picked up the case and walked toward the door.

"Thanks, Shirley." Alvarez nodded.

Alvarez turned toward me with a business card in her hand. "Your color is coming back. This can be a very traumatic experience. The report number will be available in 24 hours. Call me if you need anything."

I took the card from her and skimmed over the information. Jasmine is a name you don't hear of often. I looked at her. "Thanks."

"Stay with someone tonight and change your locks as soon as possible. Call right away if you notice anything suspicious."

The door closed behind the officers leaving a stark silence.

"This is all so weird," I said walking over to the bookshelf. And I'm not talking about the break-in. The image on the stone matching Sgt. Alvarez's tattoo is bizarre.

The stone showing me an image in the first place is weird enough. But for it to correlate with something is beyond comprehension. What does the stone want me to do with those images?

Abigail walked up behind me and placed her hands around my waist. "Why don't you come and stay at my place tonight? We can come back in the morning and clean up this mess," She said softly.

I turned and looked down at her hands, taking them off my waist. "You told me this wouldn't happen again, Abigail." I said raising my eyebrows.

"What? You think I'm coming on to you?" She shoved her hands into her hoodie pockets. "I'm just being your friend, Kristy. Honest."

"That's not the vibe I was getting from you, Abigail."

"You've made it pretty clear where we stand and I respect that. I can't even touch you as a friend?"

"Yes, you can still be friendly. My nerves are still frayed from all that's happened. I'm sorry I jumped to conclusions. " I stepped toward her and reached out my hand.

She looked at it and turned to walk out the door. "I'll wait in the car."

Damn. Why do I always mess things up?

I grabbed my keys and slammed the door behind me.

CHAPTER FIVE

Abigail dropped me off at my apartment the next morning. We talked last night and I made myself clear that we were just friends. She seemed okay with it. She also forgot she had an appointment this morning, so I'll be cleaning the apartment myself. Sleep was not my friend last night. I couldn't stop thinking about who could have broken into my place and violate me like that.

I opened the door with a childish hope the apartment was magically cleaned overnight. No such luck. Taking in the crime scene, I felt light headed and tight chested. I tossed one of the cushions onto the couch and flopped down. Resting my head against the back of the couch, I closed my eyes and took a few slow, steady breaths. Your home is supposed to be a safe haven.

"Not anymore." I looked at the books and knick-knacks strewn across the floor. "Screw it." I grabbed my keys and headed to the bar.

The office light reflected out into the hallway. I walked in and found Paige with a pencil between her teeth, money all over the desk and her right hand punching the calculator spastically.

"Hey Paige," I said, glancing at her desk.

Without looking up at me, she grunts "Hello" through the pencil.

"Last night at the bar was pretty rockin'. The real kicker was when I got home and someone broke into my place and trashed it." *That* got her attention.

Her right hand stopped mid-calculating, and she took the pencil out of her mouth. "What?"

I leaned up against my desk, took out the stone from my pocket and started playing with it. "Oh yeah... it was awesome. I love being violated in my own home," I said with a forced smile.

"Oh my god. Are you okay?"

"For the most part. Abigail came over and the police took a report. I don't know what good filing a report really does. But..." I trailed off remembering Jasmine's dragonfly tattoo. Still wondering why the stone showed me the image.

"....done something like that? You don't have any enemies do you?" Paige stared at me.

"Um." My mouth was dry and my lips stuck together. "I can't think of anyone." I licked my lips to get those few words out.

"That's crazy." She shook her head and put the pencil back in her mouth. Her fingers started where they left off on the calculator keys.

Feeling a bit woozy, I made the few steps to the couch and lay down. My eyes felt heavy and I struggled to keep them open since Paige was in the room. The next thing I knew I was back at the canyon. It was so narrow, as I walked deeper into it, I could touch both sides of the canyon with outstretched arms. The water was ankle deep and with each step the water made a 'slushing' sound.

As I came around the corner, Chief - the Native American man - sat on a large red rock formation. He motioned for me to come closer. I walked over to the rock and waited for him to say something.

"Hello Kristy. I am your Spirit Guide."

"You're my what?" My voice shrilled.

"We visit you to give you messages and protect you through life. You have many just waiting to be seen," he said, opening his arms wide. "All you have to do is be still and listen."

"Why are there many waiting for me?"

"Your process of awakening has started. There's no timeline. No right or wrong. It begins when you have shown you are ready." He placed his hands over my heart.

"How have I shown I'm ready? I've just been going through my life. Doing the same thing every day." And freaking out when weird shit like this happens.

He stood up on the rock. "Pay close attention to the people that come into your life, Kristy, for they have messages for you. The events that happen in your day-to-day life are not mundane. Be open so that your other Spirit Guides can assist you. Some have already made an appearance."

Spreading his arms out to his side, he transformed into an eagle and flew upward toward the deep blue, cloudless sky. He soared over the canyon opening. In the distance, an eagle cried.

I hear my name being called in the distance. I opened my eyes slightly to see Paige crouched beside me.

"Kristy?"

"Huh? I said, half asleep.

"You were talking in your sleep," Paige stood up.

I rolled over onto my side focusing my eyes. "Just having weird a dream."

Paige walked over to her desk and grabbed her briefcase. "I'm going to take off. Do you need anything before I go?"

"No," I mumbled.

"Okay. I'll catch ya later."

CHAPTER SIX

I walked down the hallway and paused at the end of the bar. The dim bar light reflected off the liquor bottles shining a prism of color onto the ceiling. This is the best time to be here. Standing in the middle of the empty dance floor gives me a sense of calm. The silence is peaceful.

The neon clock behind the bar brightly shows 2:00pm. I should probably clean up my apartment before it gets much later. Back in the office, I grabbed my keys and headed out to my car. Stopping abruptly, I looked around, feeling like I'm forgetting something. Patting my pockets, I make sure I have everything. My cell phone is missing.

"I must have left it inside," I said under my breath.

Back in my office, I scanned my desk, pushing papers aside. Organizing these piles keeps getting pushed down my to-do list. I wonder if it fell out of my pocket when I was lying on the couch. I looked between the cushions. Nothing. Getting down on my stomach, I swept my hand back and forth on the floor underneath the couch. The tips of my fingers hit something, but I can't quite grab it. I reached further under the couch and moved my arm toward me to see if I trapped anything.

All that I scooped up are dust bunnies. As I leaned up on my elbows, a pair of bare feet are pointed toward me. The second toe on each foot has a golden ring on them and one ankle has a bracelet of gemstones. The green, blue and red stones sparkled up at me. I stood up, following the long, shimmering blue dress. Her face is aglow, eyes twinkled and her smile is like a warm fire on a snowy day. All frantic thoughts about my lost phone have been replaced with wonder.

"Perhaps you are looking for this?" The woman says holding up a gold skeleton key.

I glanced at the key and back at her mesmerizing hazel eyes. "Um. No," I stammered. "I was actually looking for my cell phone."

The woman stepped towards me and placed the key in my palm.

"Who are you?" My eyes are transfixed to hers.

"My name is Cassandra. I'm one of your guides." She slowly closed my fingers around the key. "You might want to keep this in a safe place."

"I don't understand."

"You will soon enough."

Behind me a phone rang, making me jump. I turned and looked at the desk, and saw my cell phone under a pile of folders. The ringing stopped abruptly.

"When will I understand?" I said turning back to Cassandra. She's gone.

I ran to the office door, looked down the hallway and back up again. Empty.

My right hand is clenched tightly. As I released it, only the skeleton key reminds me that Cassandra was real.

I stood in the doorway examining it. The letters AIB are on one side with the number 14 on the other. What could it mean?

The cell phone rings again and I quickly answered it.

"Hey Abigail." My head feels fuzzy.

"Yeah. I'm good. I'll be home in a minute." I pressed the END button and shoved the key in my pocket. A "clink" sounded as it hit the stone. I rubbed my face with my hands in hopes of shaking the fogginess from my head.

"I need some fresh air," I said to no one.

"I didn't want to let myself in after what happened last night." Abigail is standing outside of my apartment.

A huge reality check hit me in the face as I opened the door.

"Ugh... I was hoping my fairy godmother stopped by while I was gone and cleaned this up." I groaned, stepped over a lamp on the floor and tossed my keys on the entrance table.

Three hours, two beers and one of my huge temper tantrums later, Abigail and I collapsed on the couch sweaty and exhausted.

"Oh, I wanted to ask you." I pulled out the gold key from my pocket. "Do you know what this belongs to? I found it under the couch in the office."

"Why were you looking under the couch?" She raised her eyebrows and took the key out of my hand.

"I was looking for my phone and the key magically appeared," I said sitting up not wanting to tell her that a mystery woman gave it to me.

Abigail turned it over. "It magically appeared, huh? It doesn't look familiar. Have you asked anyone else at the bar?"

"No." I took the key back from her. "I wonder what the letters and number signify."

"Bank or locker key, maybe?" Abigail shrugged.

"Maybe." I placed the key on the coffee table. What would AIB stand for? My thoughts scanned all the businesses one by one on the Plaza. None have those initials.

"Kristy, are you listening to me?" I hear Abigail say through my thought process.

"What?"

"I'm exhausted and it's getting late."

"Oh. Sorry," I said, snapping out of it.

Abigail stood and stretched her arms toward the ceiling.

"Thanks for your help. I couldn't have done it without you." I hugged her.

"Let's hope we don't have to do it again." She smiled and walked out the door.

Turning on my bedside lamp, I took the stone out of my pocket and as I placed it on the table and another image appeared. One that is all too familiar to me. Old Man Doom is staring up at me.

Zozobra is an annual festival in Santa Fe where people can burn the past years judgments, regrets or worries (named Old Man Doom) so that the new year is started with a clean slate.

Why would the stone be showing me Zozobra? A second image appeared when I turned the stone slightly. A hologram of a silver lighter with the letter 'Z' emerged. A sense of familiarity struck me in the gut. Where have I seen the lighter before? I moved the stone again and Old Man Doom reappeared. I keep going back and forth between the two images trying to remember.

"Wait!" I begged the stone as the images vanished.

Sinking onto the bed, I stared at the stone. This is the second set of images it has shown me. Which means it wasn't a fluke the first time. Why is the stone showing them to me at all?

I turned the stone over in my palm and rubbed the smooth surface. I need to figure out what those new images mean before something else happens. But how?

The phone beeped and a text from Randi, my bartender, appeared. I glanced at the time.

"Shoot. I lost track of time." I jammed the stone in my pocket and ran out the door.

CHAPTER SEVEN

The bar is dimly lit, empty and pleasantly quiet. My mind wandered as I placed new candles at each table and booth lining the dance floor. The images from the stone weighed heavy on my mind. None of it made sense.

A faint knock at the door snapped me out of my intense thoughts. I slowly pushed the door open, shielding my eyes from the sun's glare.

"Hi Kristy." Sergeant Alvarez took off her sunglasses and slid them down the front of her uniform shirt.

"Do you have time to talk? It'll only take a few minutes." Her thumbs were hooked on her black leather gun belt, her fingers curled between the polyester fabric of her uniform.

"Come on in." I stepped back giving her space to enter the bar. "Can I get you a drink, Officer?"

"Please, call me Jasmine. No thank you. I'm still on duty." She smiled, looking around the empty dance floor.

"It's the calm before the storm." I smiled leaning up against a table. "Is this about the break in?"

"Yes. The fingerprints came back as yours and Abigail's."

"So whoever broke in wore gloves," I said matter-of-factly.

"Possibly. There wasn't any forced entry so either the lock was picked or someone had a key." Her radio squawked and she tilted her ear toward the mic.

"Did you lock your front door that day?" she said turning the knobs on her radio.

"As far as I can remember." Doubt crept in and images from that day flashed in my mind.

"Well, double check from now on just to be safe." She glanced toward the bar and her face lit up.

Looking over my shoulder, I see Randi walking behind the bar. She has a silly grin on her face and walked our way.

"Do you know each other?" I said turning to Jasmine.

"You could say that."

Randi leaned in and kissed Jasmine on the cheek. "Hi Sweetie. What are you doing here?" She lightly touched Jasmine's hand.

"Just following up with Kristy about some business."

"Business?" Randi turned to me with raised eyebrows.

"It's no big deal." I waved her off. "Well, if that's all, I need to get back to work," I said to Jasmine.

"Here's my card if you need to contact me." Jasmine reached out her right hand. The tip of her dragonfly tattoo is visible and brings back all those feelings from the day of the break-in.

"I really should get going. Thanks for coming by." I stumbled up the hallway to the office and leaned up against Paige's desk.

I took the stone out of my pocket and turned it side by side. Nothing. It's just a regular old stone.

"Why are you showing me these images?" I yelled at it.

"Who are you talking to?" Randi appeared in the office doorway.

I jumped at the sound of her voice and quickly closed my palm around the stone. "Um. Just talking to myself. Are you going to stock the bar or should I?" The words fell out of my mouth.

"I'll do it. You relax." Randi stared at me for an uncomfortable length of time.

"Okay. I'll be down in a minute." I avoided eye contact with her, but saw her walk away in my peripheral vision.

Cradling my head in my hands, I took a deep breath. I needed to get a grip. I took another deep breath and walked back down the hallway towards the bar.

Randi has some explaining to do about Jasmine.

CHAPTER EIGHT

The fifty-foot Zozobra centered on the ritual burning of an effigy of Old Man Doom to dispel the hardships and travails of the past year. Zozobra (meaning "the gloomy one") is a yearly event in Santa Fe since 1924. It kicked off the annual Fiestas de Santa Fe. Thousands of people flock to Santa Fe to watch the giant animated wooden and cloth marionette wave its arms and groan ominously at the approach of its fate.

It's also a busy night for the Broken Chalice and we opened earlier than usual to get the celebrants juiced up before the burning begins. Abigail is taking care of deliveries while Randi and I cleaned up the bar area. I can feel the electricity of excitement in the air, which is making me restless and anxious.

"Hey Randi, do you have a lighter?" I asked placing new candles on the tables and booths.

"No, but Abigail does. She's out back." Randi pointed her thumb over her shoulder toward the alley.

Abigail is sitting on a milk crate with a cigarette in her mouth as I walked out to the alley. Her right thumb flipped the lid of a metal lighter and clicked the flint wheel, lighting the end. As she snapped the lid down, the letter "Z" appeared beneath her fingers.

My breath caught in my throat and I stopped in my tracks. I steadied myself against the doorframe.

"Hey Kristy." Abigail said through grey smoke. "What's up? You look like you've seen a ghost." She let out a deep smoker's laugh and inhaled.

"I'm fine." I finally said after moistening my parched lips. I pushed myself off the door jam and walked toward her.

"Is that your lighter?" My voice is barely audible and I cleared my throat of any nervousness.

Her lips puckered and her cheeks sunk in as she sucked on the cigarette. "My grandfather gave it to me before he died. He loved the Zorro movies so my grandmother gave him the lighter with a "Z" engraved on it. He would show it off to everyone with a long made up story about how he "knew" Zorro." Another smoker's laugh escaped her throat.

"Hmm. Interesting. In all the years we've known each other, I've never seen you with it."

She took a last drag on the cigarette, dropped it to the ground and crushed it with her foot. "It got buried during one of my moves and I found it again a few months ago rummaging through boxes in the closet." She tilted her head upward blowing the remainder of smoke toward the sky. "Why so interested?"

Do I tell her about the stone and the images it showed me? Will she even believe me since I can't actually prove it?

"It's not a big deal, really." I shrugged my shoulders.

My fingertips brushed up against the stone in my pocket.

"I've seen images in the stone and I'm not sure if they mean anything."

"What kind of images?" Abigail leaned forward, intrigued.

"Well, the first one was a dragonfly and when I moved the stone slightly, a hologram of a police shield appeared." I took out the stone and demonstrated it for her. She peered over the stone but it's blank.

"I don't see any images." Her nose wrinkled.

"They disappear shortly after showing up." I slowly put the stone back in my pocket and kept my hand around it.

Abigail continued to look at me dubiously. "I'm not imagining them," I said crossing my arms.

"So you said the first image was a dragonfly. Were there other images?"

I shuffled my feet back and forth as my heart pounded in my chest. *Should I tell her about the second images? She was already skeptical. What would she think when I told her the lighter was one of them?*

"The second image was Old Man Doom." I trailed off looking down at my feet. "I couldn't make out the hologram." The lie fell out of my mouth.

"Very fascinating. Can't say I've ever seen a stone that communicates with people." She flipped and snapped the lighter open and closed.

"That's all I've been shown," I said, gutless.

"Well, let me know if the stone sends you more messages." She stood up from the crate, shoved the lighter in her pocket and disappeared into the building, leaving me feeling sick to my stomach.

CHAPTER NINE

The bar has been packed since early evening. Randi and I are bartending while Abigail is the bar back. Zozobra has burned to oblivion and people are trickling into the streets. Abigail and I haven't spoken to each other since our conversation in the alley. Usually she loved hearing about stones and symbolism. She's the one who dragged me to gem shows because she needed to find that one gem that had magical powers. But now she's either disinterested or jealous. I can't figure out which.

A sudden sound of ice pouring into the bin startled me out of my daydreaming. I turned to see Abigail holding the ice bucket as she finished pouring and turned to go to the backroom without even a slight glance my way. Randi motioned to me that she needed change for the cash register.

I closed the office door behind me and walked toward the wall safe. My fingers barely touched the keypad when I heard a loud crash behind me. A stream of bright light that landed on the leather couch blinded me.

A "whoosh" sound and a wave of heat rushed toward me. I instinctively crouched down to my knees and, peered over Paige's desk, the couch engulfed in flames. Smoke quickly filled the room making it hard to see and breathe.

I grabbed a t-shirt from the desk chair, wrapped it around my face and got on all fours. Slowly crawling around the desk, another "whoosh" came from above. I continued to crawl towards the door. As I passed the couch, ceiling tiles collapsed causing me to fall back against the desk. Catching my breath, I reached for the door handle.

"Shit," I yelled yanking my hand away from the searing heat of the metal.

I looked over my shoulder at the flames and saw bubbles breathing on the wall. The fire is quickly devouring the bookshelf and creeping toward my desk below the broken window.

Do I have time to get to the window?

Unexpectedly, the heavy, black smoke dissipated. The window came into view and my eyes locked with the same man who stopped me from going over the cliff. He motioned me outside as a clear path to the window appeared.

I jumped onto the desk and grabbed the man's out stretched hand. He slowly pulled me through the window and as he helped me stand up, I see the name "Doc" embroidered on his shirt. I immediately made my way to the front of the bar where everyone is gathered in the street. I pulled the t-shirt off my face, coughing as my lungs invite fresh, cold air into them.

I saw "Doc" cup his ear with his hand and in the distance I hear sirens getting louder.

"How did they...?" I looked at him dazed.

Doc smiled and shrugged his shoulders.

The sirens have stopped as the fire trucks arrived at the front of the building. I ran around the corner and almost collided with a group of firefighters.

"Down there," I screamed at them, pointing at the alley.

They rushed toward the smoke and flames that were pouring out the window.

"Where's Abigail?" I shouted above the commotion as I stumbled into Randi.

"I haven't seen her," Randi yelled shrugging her shoulders.

The back door of the bar was propped open and I quickly run toward it. Just as I was about to enter the building, a firefighter stopped me.

"Abigail," I yelled past him.

"No one goes beyond this point. Ma'am, you're bleeding and need to get looked at right away," he said pointing at my hand.

I looked and saw only blood. My stomach turned and my balance wavered.

"Abigail is still in there," I pleaded with the firefighter.

He motioned for an EMT who sat me down and began bandaging the cut. I heard the firefighter send in one of his men into the building to look for Abigail.

It felt like an eternity, but the firefighter finally came into view with Abigail in tow, one ear bud from her headphones hanging down. Her face was covered in soot and she looked dazed.

I hugged her tightly exclaiming, "Oh my god, are you okay? Where were you?"

Abigail replied, "I was in the stock room with my headphones in. What the...?" She looked at my bandaged hand with wide eyes.

"It's just a small cut. I was in the office when some fool threw a Molotav cocktail into the window. Zozobra sure brings out the freaks." I pressed down the medical tape around my wrist.

"Are you the owner of this bar?" A firefighter asked me over the buzz of the continuing chaos.

"Yes. I'm Kristy."

"I'm Peter, the Fire Inspector. The fire is contained but we'll stay here a bit longer to make sure the embers don't reignite. I'll have the police officers disperse the crowd since the bar will be out of commission for a while, at least until the investigation is completed. We are treating it as a crime scene. I'll be in touch with you in the next day or two with more details. Until then, please don't enter the building."

As I thanked him, I saw Jasmine out of the corner of my eye talking to Randi and Abigail. Abigail seemed edgy, nervously looking around. She briefly made eye contact with me, said something to Randi and walked towards me. Suddenly, I am bone-weary and drained.

"Are you sure you're okay, Kristy?" Abigail gently touched my bandaged hand.

"Just exhausted," I said looking at her. "I'm so grateful that everyone got out okay. Who would want to do that to *our* bar? I mean what have we done to deserve this? It's just insane."

"I don't know, Kristy." She looked over her shoulder as the charred building was doused with water.

"Well what did that guy have to say? Did they find any clues?" Abigail crossed her arms.

"Only that it's a crime scene." Randi waved her arms in an attempt to get my attention. She motioned that she'd call me later. I gave her a thumbs up and waved goodbye.

"So that's all he said to you?" Abigail stepped closer to me.

"Yes. Abigail," I said louder than I intended.

She stepped back and put her hands up in defense. "Okay. I was only curious."

"I'm sorry. Let's get some sleep and come back tomorrow to check out the damage. Okay?" My tired eyes must have gotten the point across because her body language softened.

"Okay. I'll call you in the morning." She squeezed my arm and walked away.

Although my brain wanted to move, all I could do was stare at the stream of water cascading over the charred building. Is this what the stone was warning me about? What about the lighter? I had my theories but was too exhausted to deal with them. I slowly made my way to my car and drove off.

CHAPTER TEN

After yesterday's fire, I decided a drive would help clear my head, so I headed north to Taos. Mother Nature has a way of giving me a different perspective on life and between the break-in at my apartment and the bar fire, I needed to regroup.

On the way to Taos, my autopilot pulled to the right and headed toward Chimayo. I've been to El Santuario de Chimayo once before and found it comforting. During holy week, thousands of pilgrims walked the thirty miles from Santa Fe to the sanctuary seeking its curative powers of the "holy dirt." Maybe its healing powers will help me get some clarity on all that's been happening.

The air is crisp and fresh. A spiritual energy was felt even before I arrived at the church. Handmade crosses made of sticks and twine were tied to the metal fence that kept the horses tame. A stallion stood guard and sniffed visitors as they went by.

I gave him a gentle rub on the nose. "How ya doing, buddy?" He looked at me with wise eyes and snorted.

"You can say that again." I rubbed his nose again and continued walking up the path toward the church.

A stone wall lines the pathway. Stained glass windows of a rose, heart, and cross guided me closer. A courtyard to the right had gorgeous wooden benches forming an outside church, facing a dark wooden altar.

Beyond the altar is a shrine of Our Lady of Guadalupe. Colorful rosaries hang from her outstretched arms and flowers and candles cover her feet. To the right of the altar is a row of seven large crosses made of stone. As with the metal fence and shrine, handmade crosses, rosaries, and flowers leaned against them.

After pausing in the courtyard, I sat down on one of the wooden benches. A word was engraved on each of them: Peace. Wisdom. Light. Transformation. Choice. After a few moments the crowd of people grew bigger, but the noise level stayed quiet. It was an unspoken rule that people respected the grounds as sacred and holy. A light breeze rustled the trees nearby and caressed my face. I closed my eyes taking a few deep breaths until my body sank into the wood. Opening my eyes, I saw Chief staring at me.

Did I fall asleep on the bench? I looked around at the people in the courtyard. *No, I'm still awake. Why is he sitting in front of me as if he is real?* I reached out and touched his knee. I quickly pulled my hand back when I felt the soft leather of his pants.

"Are you for real?" I whispered leaning toward him.

"Yes, I am," he whispered back, mimicking me.

"What are you doing here?" I asked under my breath, in case I'm the only one that could see him.

"I'm just letting you know that I'm here in case you need any help in paying attention to those messages that come your way today."

"I'm too exhausted to deal with this spiritual guide stuff today," I said looking around. "I'm sure there's someone else here that you can go be a spirit guide to."

He tilted his head back and let out a hearty laugh.

"Shhhhhh! I don't want people to hear you," I said grabbing his arm.

"Don't worry, Kristy, you're the only one who can hear me." He's still catching his breath after laughing so hard.

"So why can I see you in real life this time and not in a dream? Why do you feel like just another person sitting here having a conversation?"

He looked directly into my eyes and took my hands. "Because I wanted you to know that I am real."

I looked down at our hands and then up at him. "I know I've been told to be aware of signs in my life and pay attention to the events that happened to me. But I can't make sense of them. I don't know why my apartment got ransacked or why the bar was targeted or why the stone shows images." My face felt hot and tears stung my eyes.

"There is a message in everything that happens. Listen to that quiet voice inside of you." He squeezed my hand.

A group of people walked past me chanting something I couldn't make out. I turned to look at Chief, but he was gone. I glanced around the courtyard and the path up to the church but I didn't see him.

"I just love our little chats!" I yelled to the blue sky.

People looked my way and I half smiled at them. I walked up to the church and made my way to the entrance, pausing in the foyer. The church was sparsely lit. The altar was wood painted in gold, red, blue, and green. A wooden box with a heart painted on it sat in the middle of the table. To the right of the altar were prayer candles that visitors had lit in memory of a loved one or a prayer they wanted answered.

I walked over to the candles, struck a match and while lighting the wick, wished that the strange events in my life would stop happening. I stared intently at the flame for a few seconds to emphasize my wish.

I sat at the far end of the front row pew and took in all the symbolism on the altar. Images from the stone flashed in my mind. The dragonfly, shield, Zozobra, the lighter.

The lighter...who set the bar on fire? Are the images pointing me to someone or something?

My chest tightened and I realized I'm holding my breath. Feeling restless, my eyes darted around the room looking for an escape from my thoughts. I see a glimpse of Doc standing inside the brightly lit doorway. He motioned me to join him.

Out in the warm sunshine, Doc guided me to the wall over-looking the courtyard and pointed down at the altar. I turned to him and shrugged. This time he exaggerated his finger pointing toward the table. I leaned over the wall to get a closer look at what he was pointing at and saw the letters A-I-B in the center of the wooden table.

"Where have I seen those letters before?" I asked looking over my shoulder.

He had vanished, leaving me talking to myself once again. What is it with the guides leaving so abruptly? A heavy sigh escaped my lungs.

I make my way down the path to the parking lot as the sun dips behind the mountainside. My phone rang as I reached the horses.

"Hello?" I whispered.

"Kristy, it's Peter with the fire department. I have some information regarding the fire. Can we meet at the bar right away?" His voice is calm, yet urgent.

"I'll be there as soon as I can." I hung up and jogged to my car.

CHAPTER ELEVEN

A red SUV with a large SFFD emblem on the driver's side door came into view as I turned into the bar parking lot. In the side mirror, Peter, the inspector, jumped out of the vehicle as I turned off the engine. I almost didn't recognize him without his oversized jacket and helmet.

He looked more relaxed in his blue uniform and black work boots carrying a clipboard and walkie-talkie.

He walked toward me with an outstretched hand as I stepped out of my car. "Hi, Kristy." He shook my hand with a smile.

"Hey Peter. Sorry for taking so long. I got here as fast as I could."

"No problem at all. It's a nice day for a drive. Let's walk down the alley. There's something I want to show you."

We stepped over charred wood and murky puddles as we walked toward the office window. The smell of wet, burnt wood found its way to my nose.

"Phew," I say covering my face with my shirt.

"You get used to it," Peter said stopping in front of what is now a large piece of plywood nailed to the window frame.

"So in the office we found a broken bottle with a charred rag near it. The rag was covered in an accelerant. Probably gasoline. Someone lit the rag soaked with gasoline and threw it through the window."

The startling crack of glass breaking and the flash of light as the fire ignited clouded my head. My throat felt dry from the smell of gas and thick smoke.

"Any fingerprints on the bottle?" I said clearing my throat of the memory.

"Not on the bottle. But we did find a couple partial prints around the window. We'll need fingerprints from you and your staff to see if any match."

I nodded, breathing through my shirt.

"We also found this in the alley." Peter slides an 8x10 photo out of a manila envelope. "Does this look familiar to you?"

My stomach dropped and my hand reached for the wall when my knees gave out.

"Easy there," Peter said grabbing my elbow. "Are you feeling okay?"

"Oh my god." I said under my breath, holding the shirt to my face even tighter.

"So you have seen this before." He held up the photo of Abigail's silver lighter. It's scuffed and black with the "Z" tarnished.

I hold the photo a few inches in front of me. My mind is racing. Why would Abigail's lighter be considered evidence? Would she set the bar on fire? There's no way she would do this to her own business. To *our* business.

"Kristy," Peter said snapping me out of my trance.

"It's Abigail's but there's no way she could be part of this." I handed him back the photo.

"We don't know for sure that she's involved. We found it by the dumpster."

I looked over his shoulder at the dirty blue steel box with the letters of Waste Management partially scraped off. The milk crate Abigail sat on rested up against it.

"She takes cigarette breaks out here sometimes so maybe she dropped it." I say rationalizing my worst fears.

"That could very well be the case. I'll have to ask her about it." He slid the photo back inside the envelope. "When would be a good time to get your employees fingerprints?"

Still staring at the dumpster and reliving the conversation with Abigail the night of the fire, I slowly came out of my stupor.

"I'll call everyone to meet tomorrow." I pushed myself off the wall and walked toward the parking lot.

"I'll be at the station all day," Peter said opening the driver side door, tossing his clipboard onto the seat.

My phone rang and I waved goodbye to Peter as I answered it.

It's Jasmine.

"Hi. Do you have any new information about the break-in?" I opened the car door and slid behind the wheel.

"No. I'm calling about Paige." I can hear loud voices and music in the background.

"Paige?" I turned the key in the ignition and started backing out of the parking spot.

"She's sitting in the Plaza and I think she's had too much to drink. Can you come down?"

"I'm on my way." My tires screeched as I pulled out of the parking lot.

CHAPTER TWELVE

I found parking near the Orr house and walked to the center of the Plaza. Jasmine waved, from the sidewalk of the Palace of Governors where Native Americans sold handmade jewelry made of silver and turquoise. As I crossed the street I spotted Paige sitting on the curb, rocking back and forth and muttering.

I smiled at Jasmine and squatted down in front of Paige.

"Hey Paige." I put my hands on her knees.

"Kristy!" Paige practically shouted, as if she hadn't seen me in years. "What are you doing here?"

"I came to take you home."

"I don't want to go home. I want to sit here." Paige patted the curb next to her for emphasis.

I looked up at Jasmine. "You don't have to stay. I can get her to my car."

"She's pretty drunk. You might need my help." Jasmine stepped beside Paige. "Let's stand her up and see how she does."

We each grabbed Paige under one arm and pulled her up on her feet. Paige started tipping over but Jasmine grabbed her around the waist.

"Easy does it," Jasmine said, steadying Paige.

"Dizzy. Need to sit down." Paige rolled her head from side to side.

"Let's go for a walk, Paige." Jasmine motioned me toward the park.

We made it to the bandstand before Paige slurred that she needed to puke. We dove for the nearest trashcan and I held her hair back while she heaved up the contents of her stomach. Tourists enjoying their day in the park scrambled away from the retching sounds.

"Ugh." Paige spit and wiped her mouth with the back of her hand.

"All done?" I asked.

She rested her head on the arm hugging the trashcan. "I did a horrible thing."

"You just threw up, Paige. That's not horrible."

"It was bad. Really bad." She slurred, swaying back and forth.

I glanced over at Jasmine who shrugged in response.

"What are you talking about, Paige?" I leaned down next to her face.

"I'm a terrible person." Paige threw up again.

"You're going to be okay," I said pulling her hair back behind her ear.

While I waited for Paige to collect herself I looked across the Plaza toward the La Fonda hotel, and a sign caught my eye. The sign featured only three letters: A-I-B.

"Holy shit," I said under my breath.

"What?" Jasmine looked at me with one eyebrow arched.

I regained my composure. "It's nothing. I thought I saw someone I knew, but it's not them." I put my hand on Paige's shoulder. "How're you doing? Ready to walk to the car?"

Paige didn't answer, so I bent down to look at her face. "She seems to have passed out."

"I knew you'd need my help." Jasmine grinned.

We propped Paige up between us and walked her back to my car. Bystanders gawked at the spectacle, but I avoided eye contact and focused on one step at a time. We arrived at my car and buckled Paige in the front passenger seat. She stirred a bit, but kept her eyes closed.

"Thanks for your help," I said as I tucked Paige's feet in and closed the door. "I'm sure Paige appreciates it too."

"Glad I was there to intercept any cops that might have found her. She would not have liked spending the night in a jail cell."

"You'd be right about that." I nodded. "I'll take her to my place for the night so I can keep an eye on her."

"Call if you need anything."

We said our goodbyes and I drove through the Plaza. My thoughts drifted to the AIB sign and if it had anything to do with the key.

As I pulled into my parking spot at the apartment complex Paige opened her eyes slightly. "Where am I?"

"Oh, look. Sleeping beauty has awoken."

She groaned and rested her head against the window.

"Don't move too fast. I don't need you barfing in my car." I quickly walked around the front of the car and opened the side door.

"Don't be mean." Paige slurred as she swung her legs out of the car.

"Whoa." She shot her arms out to hold onto the door and me.

"Take your time."

Paige took a few deep breaths. "Okay. Ready." She slowly stood up. "Oh boy."

I held my hand out for her to grab onto. She could explain her bender later.

CHAPTER THIRTEEN

Cassandra stood standing in a meadow of giant yellow sunflowers. Her arms hung by her side, palms out, her face tilted toward the sky. The light breeze gently rustled her dress and the towering sunflowers swayed back and forth. As I walked closer, a rainbow of colors pulsated around Cassandra's body. I stopped a few feet away, not to disturb her.

"I've been waiting for you," Cassandra said reaching out her hands to me.

I took her hands in mine as an intense orange glow emanated from her chest, flowed down her arms and into her hands. An intense feeling of déjà vu overcame me.

"Where are we?" I looked around in wonder at the vast meadow.

"This is where you stayed prior to being born."

"*Before* being born? How is that possible?" I said holding my hand up as if to somehow stop the madness.

"Your soul remembers, Kristy. It remembers all of the places." Cassandra scanned the sky and inhaled deeply. "It's time *you* remember."

I ran my fingers through a group of daisies and buttercups trying to process that I was here before.

"The place isn't the significant part of this journey. It's what you decided here that really matters. I'm only here to remind you of what you agreed to do with the life you are living now."

"What I agreed to do?" I said with raised eyebrows.

"When you decided to be born into this lifetime, you made a sacred agreement. You agreed to do certain things, meet certain people, learn certain lessons, and give of your gifts. And you were given many gifts, Kristy. It is my honor to remind you of them and make sure you are following the path that was designed especially for you."

My mind raced. Sacred agreement? Gifts? Why couldn't I remember?

"Everyone has a path. Some people know what that path is. Others do not. You may not realize it, but you put the call out for your guides to help. That is why Doc and Chief made themselves known to you."

"You know each other?"

"Your spirit guides are interconnected. Think of us as your private line to the divine." Cassandra chuckled at her own rhyme.

I walked a few steps into the golden meadow and looked toward the horizon. All I could see was flowers for miles.

Why would I want to leave this place? What could possibly have pulled me away?

"You knew the importance of your gifts and the urgency that people on earth needed to experience them," Cassandra said as if answering my questions.

She guided me to a grove of tall, enormous sunflowers and pulled one closer to us. An image of a glowing yellow orb appeared in the center of the flower. It's floating above the same meadow where I'm standing. A woman walked up and placed her hands on either side of the orb.

"Is that you?" I said pointing to the flower.

"Yes, and that is you in my hands."

I felt the orb's vibration enter my solar plexus and a warm sensation traveled through my body. My breath caught in my throat, my vision blurred and my head was woozy. Losing my balance, Cassandra quickly grabbed me by the waist, pulling me close to her. The vibration subsided and my eyes refocused on the sunflower.

"This was the moment when your soul agreed to live on earth and share its gifts." She squeezed me tighter.

Tears trickled down my cheeks as I watched Cassandra kiss the orb, releasing it in the air. She smiled and bowed as it floated away.

The sun shined warm beams of light on me through the bedroom curtains. Am I still dreaming? Sounds from the kitchen gave me a reality check but I can't shake how real the dream felt. I see sunflower petals on the sheets as I threw back the covers.

"What the?" I exclaimed picking one up. Holding it to my nose, I inhaled the flower essences of the meadow. A knock at the door startled me and the petal slipped out of my fingers.

"Coffee's ready," Paige said on the other side of the door.

"Be out in a second."

I slowly swung my legs over the edge of the bed and placed the petal next to the stone sitting on the bedside table. An image appeared on the stone and I picked it up to get a closer look. A Saab logo shined up at me. Moving the stone side to side, another image came through.

It's some sort of tool. Looking closer, I realized that it's a bartender's tool that is similar to a Leatherman.

The images slowly disappeared and the stone returned to its natural state. I wrote down the images in my journal, briefly glancing at the previous images shown to me.

What would a Saab and Leatherman tool have to do with each other? What about the other images? Are they related?

The events of the last few months flashed quickly one after the other in my mind. It was all crashing in on me and I was about to break. The hike, accident, break-in, bar fire, Chief and Cassandra. Abigail and her lighter. The Saab.

I own a Saab. What if something happens to me in my car? My heart skipped a beat.

My feet touched the carpet but my legs are shaky and weak. My hands are clammy and my breathing is shallow. I fell back onto the bed and looked at the stone. The Saab emblem and Leatherman tool faded away.

If the images are warning me of things to come, how am I supposed to prepare for the new images? Maybe Paige can help me figure it out.

CHAPTER FOURTEEN

Paige stood in the kitchen sipping coffee and staring into space. I watched her from the hallway for a few minutes and she didn't blink or move her eyes during that time.

"How are you feeling this morning?" I said as I walked into the kitchen.

It took Paige a second to snap out of it and reply. "A little under the weather." Her eyes are red and there's a scent of alcohol exuding from her body.

After pouring myself a cup of coffee, I motioned her to the couch and we sat down.

"Do you remember anything that happened yesterday in the Plaza?" I said looking over the mug at her as I took a drink.

"I remember getting there and sitting on the sidewalk. Why? Did I do something embarrassing?" Paige clutched her necklace.

"Well, besides having to be carried out of the Plaza, no, you didn't do anything embarrassing," I said smirking at her.

Paige sighed and looked down at her hands holding the mug.

"Jasmine helped me get you to the car."

"Jasmine was there?" Paige's cheeks flushed pink.

"She called me to come and get you. She saved your ass from getting arrested."

Paige slumped down into the couch and covered her face with her hands. "Oh my god."

"There is one thing I want to ask you about something you said yesterday."

"What did I say?" She looked up at me with scared, wide eyes.

"You said that you did a horrible thing and that you're a terrible person. Was it because you felt terrible for getting drunk or because you actually did do something terrible?"

Paige stared straight ahead for a good ten to fifteen seconds before placing her mug on the coffee table. The sound of the ceramic mug hitting the glass top echoed sharply through the living room. Her chest heaved up and down, possibly getting up enough courage to answer the question.

"It ripped my world apart." She finally whispered.

I wanted to ask her what "it" was but decided to give her the time to explain on her own. It was obvious that this was difficult enough without me pressuring her for details.

"Yesterday was the tenth anniversary of his death." Paige could barely get the words out. Her body convulsed with deep sobs, escaping out of her mouth in long wailing sounds.

She collapsed into me as I put my arm around her shoulder in an attempt to comfort her. "I'm so sorry, Paige," I said not knowing what happened or to whom.

"He was only five." She sobbed uncontrollably.

Rocking her back and forth, her sobbing slowed down to a whimper. I handed her a box of tissues and she wiped the wetness from her face and nose.

Waiting in the heavy silence, an image comes to mind of when Paige joined the Broken Chalice team as the bookkeeper. The first few months she didn't go into the bar area, she only stayed in the office and always used the back entrance.

As she seemed to get more comfortable, Paige would visit us at the bar counter as we were getting ready to open. She didn't stay long and she turned down offers of drinks. I didn't think too much about it at the time, but looking back it all makes sense.

The sound of Paige blowing her nose brought me back to the present.

"We don't need to talk about this if you don't want to, Paige." I took a drink of lukewarm coffee.

"I want to. I *need* to." She stood up, raising her mug. "More coffee first."

"Good idea." I followed her into the kitchen. Paige refilled our mugs and leaned up against the counter.

"I'm an alcoholic, Kristy." Paige looked deep into her mug.

"Honestly, it didn't occur to me. I'm sorry I wasn't more aware."

"I've had many years of sobriety, until yesterday." Her eyes welled up as she sipped her coffee.

Not knowing what to say, I walked over and hugged her.

"It's okay, Kristy." Paige patted my back and I took that as a cue to let go.

"This isn't the first time I've fallen off the wagon. I guess one can hold it together for only so long."

"My husband was working a night shift the day it happened," Paige whispered. "I got off work early to pick up Jimmy, my son, from school." Her eyes stared straight ahead at the memory. "We had our ritual of going to the candy store on the way home. He loved sour gummy worms." She smiled, but a tear slid down her cheek.

"He ate his favorite dinner of hot dogs and mac and cheese. He loved to slide the noodles onto each of the fork prongs and eat them. I had my favorite dinner of four martinis. After his nightly bath, Jimmy went into this room to play with Legos until it was bedtime."

Paige slowly turned to face the sink, poured out the coffee and set the mug on the counter. "I'm sorry. You probably need to get to the bar. I can leave so you can start your day."

"I don't have to be anywhere, Paige. Let's sit down." I pointed to the kitchen table. Her movements were slow and sorrowful.

"I'm here to listen to as much as you want to tell me." I touched her forearm lightly.

"Only one other person knows what happened. You deserve to know after yesterday." Paige looked down at her trembling hands.

"So, Jimmy was in his room and I was on the couch doing my usual night ritual of cocktails and T.V. I must have fallen asleep because the next thing I remember was waking up smelling smoke and coughing. It took me a second to realize I wasn't dreaming. The room was filled with smoke and the heat from the flames hit my face as soon as I stood up."

Following her eyes to the table, I see she has shredded a few sheets of tissue.

"The smoke was so thick. I crouched down on the floor and crawled to the hallway. My eyes stung and my throat burned with every step. Jimmy's room was at the end of the hall."

Paige covered her face with her hands. Sobs escaped from her throat and tears fell onto the table.
"I'm so sorry." I placed my hand on her shoulder. Tears blurred my vision.

"The firefighters busted through the front door and tried to grab me but I fought them off because I had to get to him. I was screaming and pointing that Jimmy was down the hall but they couldn't understand me. They carried me outside. I was still screaming at them that my son was inside." Her face was flushed and wet with tears.

"The fire was too much even for them." Paige sighed and shook her head. "It's all my fault."

"I'm sure it wasn't your fault, Paige."

"They said it was an electrical fire in the back of the house. The wiring was faulty."

"Then it wasn't your fault, Paige. It was an accident." I squeezed her hand.

"He would still be alive if I wasn't passed out on the couch. I wish it were me that died in that fire, not him. He was innocent and had his whole life ahead of him." Paige dabbed her eyes with a tissue.

A knock at the door startled both of us.

"Who could that be?" I said sliding my chair across the floor. Opening the door, Abigail pushed past me.

"I've been calling you all morning. Why haven't you called me back?" Abigail stopped abruptly by the couch, facing me. Her face is beet red with visibly pulsing neck veins.

"What's so urgent that you need to barge into my apartment?" My voice echoed off the walls.

"I need to know what the inspector said about the fire. You haven't told me anything." Her eyes are wide and her arms are flailing.

I walked past her and stopped behind Paige at the kitchen table. "Paige and I have been talking over coffee."

"Oh...Hi Paige." Abigail gestured a small wave. "I didn't realize..." She stepped back. "Is everything okay?" She said still looking at Paige dabbing her eyes.

"Everything is fine," I said with a clenched jaw. "We'll talk later at the bar."

"It's okay, Kristy." Paige said getting up from the table. "I need to get going anyway." She gathered the shredded tissue and walked into the kitchen.

"Paige, you don't have to leave. We haven't finished talking," I said following her.

"You've done so much already, Kristy. Thank you." Paige grabbed her purse from the couch and opened the front door.

"Call me anytime." I hugged her. "I'm here for you." Paige's lips quivered into a semi-smile.

"What is wrong with you?" I said to Abigail after closing the door.

Abigail shrugged her shoulders. "I'm sorry."

"We've known each other for a long time and you haven't been yourself lately. What's going on?" I stepped closer to her.

"Well, it's been very stressful with everything happening at the bar." Abigail trailed off.

"That's it? Stress is making you act crazy?" I chuckled in disbelief. "You aren't telling me everything."

"I feel out of the loop regarding the fire. It's my business too and I have a right to know." Abigail's voice boomed.

"They haven't told me much, Abigail. It's an ongoing investigation."

Abigail looked at me with wild, darting eyes. She's fidgeting with her car keys.

"I will tell you this. I just found out your lighter with the "Z" engraved on it was found in the aftermath of the fire. Anything you want to tell me about that?" I said taking a step closer to her.

She immediately crossed her arms across her chest. "I smoke in the alley. You know that."

"Who said it was found in the alley?" I said trying to call her bluff.

"Kristy, I had nothing to do with the fire. You have to believe me," Abigail said not missing a beat.

"I thought I knew you after all these years, but I'm not so sure anymore. I have no doubt the fire inspector will find out who started the fire and how." I raised my eyebrows.

Abigail stepped toward me. "I promise I had nothing to do with it," she said spreading her hands as if wiping something away.

"Now if we are done here, I have things to do." I opened the front door and motioned for Abigail to leave.

She stared at me as she walked out. I heard her shout, "I didn't do it" as I closed the door behind me.

CHAPTER FIFTEEN

The Plaza was busy for a weekday. Food vendors and artists peddled their wares while buskers played their hearts out for small change. I parked on Water Street and walked to the La Fonda hotel. The sign was near a street lamp, with the letters AIB engraved into wood hanging from metal chains. My eyes followed an arrow next to the letters that pointed up. The second floor window was covered to keep wandering eyes from looking in.

A group of tourists surrounded me as they waited for the white glo-brite figure on the stoplight to grant them permission to cross the street. I pushed my way through the group and stopped at the entryway where a directory listed merchants. AIB wasn't there. I doubled checked to make sure I didn't miss it in my haste.

Walking back out to the sidewalk, I looked to the left of the entrance to see if there was a separate door. Finding nothing but a solid wall, I stepped up into the entryway.

My eyes adjusted to the darkness and a black wooden door appeared to the right of the directory. I pulled on the black metal doorknob but the door didn't budge. Making sure it wasn't stuck, I tugged on it a second time with no luck.

As I turned around to walk away, I noticed a doorbell on the side of the wall. I pushed the beige button with my forefinger, but no sound followed. I pressed it a couple more times in hopes I would hear some kind of chime emanate from inside the door.

"Who is it?" A deep voice boomed in an English accent.

I gasped and jumped back.

"Is someone there?" The mysterious Englishman asked.

"Um, yes. I'm here," I stuttered.

"What do you want?"

I combed my fingers through my hair, took a deep breath and mustered up enough nerve to answer.

"I...um...wanted to talk to someone about...AIB?" My voice cracked.

"Who's asking?"

Who is this, the Wizard of Santa Fe? I didn't have the nerve to say it out loud.

"My name is Kristy. You don't know me, but I saw your sign and it matched a key..." I cut myself off.

Maybe I shouldn't have mentioned the key.

"Key?" The deep voice had gone up an octave. "What key?"

"Um….well…"

I could walk away and never come back. Act as if the key never existed. No one would even know.

I looked up at the ceiling, relieved that there weren't any cameras pointed down at me.

"The cameras aren't up there." The deep voice replied back.

My heart skipped a beat and I could feel my face flush. Turning toward the street, Chief was leaning against a streetlamp. He smiled and waved. I put both my hands up and shrugged as if to say, now what? Chief motioned for me to turn around. I dropped my hands and waited for a second option. He repeated the motion and walked out of sight around the corner. So much for my guides helping me in times of distress.

"Do you want to come in and talk? Or are you just going to stand there?" The voice was growing impatient.

"Uh...sure."

The door buzzed open, and I entered into a small foyer.

"Go up the stairs and enter the door on the right," the voice instructed.

My nerves slowly led me up the long wooden staircase. I used the banister for support. When I finally reached the landing, I realized I was holding my breath. I walked into another small foyer and attempted to calm myself down by inhaling deeply.

"Walk down the hallway and have a seat on the couch." The booming voice said from speakers above.

The hallway was short and narrow with empty walls. Its wood-planked floors felt solid below my feet and the room was dead silent. As I crouched down on to the couch, a section of the wall slid open and a robust well-dressed man emerged. His dark hair was sleek and perfectly placed and his moustache was curled perfectly on both sides of his lips. A gold chain rested against his stomach and disappeared behind his plaid jacket. I jumped up and wiped my clammy hands on the back of my jeans. The man stopped at the side of the chair in front of me and clasped his hands behind his back.

"You wanted to talk about a key you found?" he said.

"Yes. Where am I?" I looked around the spotless room.

"My name is Ambrose. Do you have the key with you?" He asked looking down at my hands.

"Um, no."

"Well, what good is a key if you don't have it with you?"

"Right," I said looking down like a scolded child.

"Where did you find the key?"

"At my business."

"And you're sure it has the initials AIB on it?"

"Yes," I said with conviction. "What does AIB stand for?"

"I need proof that you have the key before I answer that question. Come back tomorrow at the same time. Bring the key." Ambrose turned and walked toward the door-wall.

"Um..."

He stopped and looked over his shoulder. "Yes?"

"Who should I ask for when I come back tomorrow?"

"Simply ring the doorbell," he said, and then disappeared behind the door as it melted into the wall.

I hurried out of the office, down the stairs and out to the street. Getting in my car, I attempted to put the key in the ignition but they dropped on the floor from my hands shaking.

This is nuts. I can't come back tomorrow.

"You must come back, Kristy. The key is the answer," Chief said from the passenger seat.

"I'm too scared about what might happen." My head fell onto the steering wheel.

Chief cupped my trembling hand with both of his. "You don't have a choice. This is crucial to your journey. You have to do it." He released my hand and got out of the car.

My whole body was trembling now and my mind was racing. I couldn't decide whether I wanted to run as far as I could or trust Chief. As if on autopilot, I reached for my keys, started the car and drove away from the curb.

CHAPTER SIXTEEN

Sleep eluded me after yesterdays meet and greet at AIB. I was hoping the three cups of coffee and the cold, day-old burrito would help with the nervous excitement coursing through my body but no such luck. I decided I couldn't put it off any more. I shoved the key and stone into my pants pocket, and closed the door behind me.

As I walked up to my car, I saw the driver side back tire was flat. I crouched down and carefully brushed my hand along the top of the tire. My fingertips stopped at a large gouge on the back of it.

"Crap. Just what I don't need today." I looked behind the tire to get a better look and saw a long, thin piece of metal on the ground. I realized that it looks like part of a

Leatherman tool. Immediately, my thoughts go to the stone and the last two images it showed.

A Saab logo and a Leatherman tool. So it was telling me something. But who would cut my tire on purpose?

I popped the trunk and put the contents on the ground then lifted the cover and took out the spare. Luckily, it's in good condition and I've had practice changing a tire in the past.

With the spare tire on and the piece of metal I found in my glove box, I finally pulled out of the parking lot and headed toward the Plaza.

The Bite of Santa Fe, an event where local wineries, restaurants and breweries showcased their wares for the public to sample, was happening at the convention center. So I ended up having to park five blocks from the Plaza.

The brisk walk helped burn off some of my nervous energy. I crossed Lincoln Avenue and passed a popcorn vendor and a busker on a wooden crate channeling Jimi Hendrix. I cut across the Plaza and walked over the plaque that declared that spot to be the end of the Santa Fe Trail.

A woman walked toward me as I approached the corner of San Francisco Street and Palace Avenue. I tried to move around her to cross the street, but she mirrored my movement and I stopped abruptly.

"Excuse me," I said touching her elbow to coax her to move aside.

"I can't allow you to go there," the gangly, dark haired woman warned as she grabbed my hand.

Her bony fingers and the coldness of her touch went through me. "I'm sorry?" I said pulling my hand away.

"Don't sell your soul, Kristy."

"How do you know my name?" I stared her down.

"I'm warning you...what you're about to do is a big mistake." She stared back, unblinking.

"Have we met before?" The woman's dark black hair covered half of her face but her mesmerizing green eyes reminded me of the night at the bar when a similar looking woman with a crystal around her neck talked to me.

She gave me a sinister glance and pressed her dark cloak collar around her neck. "The man you're about to do business with is not interested in what's best for you."

"How do you know I'm going to see a man?" I stepped back and stood up straight.

She cowered deeper into her cloak but then as if a spring was released, her head popped out. "I know many things about you, Kristy." Her eyes glowed and her fingers twitched.

"It was you at the bar that night. Only your hair was blonde, but those eyes..." I leaned in closer to her. "You were more pleasant then too."

"Humph." She pulled her cloak tighter around her body and walked past me. "Don't say I didn't warn you."

After making sure she didn't follow me, I walked across Water Street and stopped in front of the dark wooden door of AIB. I breathed deeply and pressed the doorbell.

CHAPTER SEVENTEEN

The door buzzed open, and I started my ascension into the unknown. My right hand guided me as it slid up the smooth wooden banister. Opening the door on the right at the top of the stairs, I entered the empty foyer and sat on the couch.

This time I eased back into the cushions and watched the wall where the door had appeared the day before. Sensing someone behind me, I turned around to see Ambrose looking down at me. He wore a crisp white collared shirt with a dark tie, tweed jacket and professionally pressed pants.

"You were expecting someone else?"

"No. I was expecting you to come through that wall." I stood up and pointed to the opposite seamless oak wall.

"Follow me." He stopped abruptly and looked me in the eye. "You do have the key, I presume?"

"Yes," I said with a shaky voice.

"Good. Come this way."

Ambrose led me down a narrow hallway, his shoulders almost touching the sides of the wall. The only sound was our footsteps on the carpeted floors. Finally, the hallway opened up into a large dark room with two reclining chairs in the center. I looked up to see a black domed ceiling with small lights rimming the bottom edge.

The room reminded me of my high school planetarium. I loved leaning back in the old plastic chairs and losing myself in the fake constellations and planets. Even though it was a fake universe, it still made me feel part of something much bigger. The booming voice of the teacher and the sound of the motor when the sky would rotate always kept me grounded to earth.

A podium stood in front of the chairs. On top of it was a red button the size of a silver dollar protected by a clear plastic cover. A keyhole and number pad sat next to the button. Seeing all this gave me the feeling of coming home, which calmed my nerves and steadied my breath. I felt like I'd been here before. Maybe not in this exact room, but I couldn't shake the feeling that something was very familiar about where I stood.

"We need to discuss some business." Ambrose's voice snapped me out of my déjà vu.

He stood by the chair closest to the podium, with one hand on the headrest and the other in his jacket pocket.

"Business?"

"The key, Kristy." He raised his hand.

I could barely breathe. How did the familiar, calm, homey feeling turn to fear, dread and confusion so fast?

My eyes darted around the room to find a quick exit, but the way we'd come in was now a solid wall, like in the first room. And unlike my high school planetarium, there weren't any neon exit signs leading me to freedom.

In my panic to get out, I caught sight of a row of chairs to the right. I walked over and slowly sat down. I took a couple deep breaths in hopes of calming my nerves.

"It's okay, Kristy. Everyone has the same reaction," Ambrose said. His attempt did not reassure me.

I gave him a dirty look through the web of my fingers. "That's comforting."

He walked over and clasped his hands in front of his substantial stomach. "Do you need more time to collect yourself or are you ready to proceed?"

I shifted in my seat and rubbed the back of my neck as I let out a shaky breath.

"I will take that to mean you need more time."

"Wait," I mumbled. I stood up and stretched my arms in front of me.

Ambrose stood to the side, bowing and motioning me to lead the way.

I walked over to one of the reclining chairs. The smell of the leather wafted upward as I caressed the sleek black armrest. An image of my first new car flashed in my mind and made my mouth curve into a smile. My Ford Mustang Coupe, what a beauty. This chair even had a seat belt, and I wondered where it would take me.

"That is for your safety," he said.

"Is this some kind of ride?"

Ambrose shrugged. "In some way I suppose it is." He picked lint off his sleeve.

"I have a few questions I want answered before we go any further." I crossed my arms.

"As I suspected." He motioned me to sit down.

"No thanks. I'd rather stand." I wasn't ready to buckle up just yet.

Ambrose nodded and clasped both hands behind his back.

"Who are you and what will you do with the key?"

"You don't beat around the bush, do you?"

I stared at him, raising my eyebrows as a prompt.

"First of all, you came to me. Second, who I am is not important. Lastly, the key can be utilized to bring forth the light that is already inside you. However," he pointed his finger to the ceiling, "you must stay open to the experience."

"So you're saying the key will enlighten me?"

"Enlightened is such a, well, powerful word, Kristy. Only a select few are deemed worthy of experiencing that level of spirituality. I am sorry to inform you that you have not been chosen."

"So if I wasn't chosen, why did I find the key?" I smirked at him.

Ambrose took a breath and looked skyward. "Let me make this simple for you. You must answer two questions, the first being: Are you ready to use the key to continue on the path you are meant to walk? And second, are you open to receiving the information it will unveil?"

"Can I think about it and come back tomorrow?" I knew I was pushing my luck.

He thought about it for a moment, and then shook his head.

Over Ambrose's shoulder I saw movement at the back of the room. I peered through the darkness but couldn't make out the figure. Out of the shadows came a black cowboy hat with a silver studded band. Doc's face lit up and he grinned. Relieved to see him, I grinned back, but realized that Ambrose is probably wondering what I'm smiling about. So, I played it cool and rested my arm on the headrest of the chair.

"So, um, I have to decide right now?" I stalled, waiting for a signal from Doc.

"Yes."

Doc fiddled with something around his neck. He pulled a long chain out from under his shirt, and held up the object that hung from it.

It was a golden skeleton key.

Doc pointed to the key and then pointed back at me. I nodded to let him know I understood. He stepped back into the darkness and disappeared.

Taking the key out of my pocket, I turned it over and over. I wished for more time to decide, but knew I didn't have it.

Did I go with Doc's advice or leave?

"Your transformation will occur regardless of your decision today. Your experience with the key may quicken the process compared to doing it on your own," Ambrose said sensing my hesitation. "There is no point in trying to control how long it might take. Your heart and soul connection will dictate how it transpires."

"Heart and soul connection?" I crinkled my nose. "How can a key do that?"

Ambrose pulled and twisted his mustache. The curled ends snapped back into place when he released them.

"What you are asking does not have a clear cut answer. There is no definite in the infinite."

I shuffled my feet back and forth as I stared at the key.

Ambrose rubbed his neck and looked up at the night sky gleaming from the dome. "Perhaps you are not as ready as I presumed."

"It's just..." I glanced around the room. "This is all happening so fast." My eyes burned with tears and I quickly wiped them away.

"The speed in which something occurs is based on one's perception. You seemed prepared yesterday, but now that you are actually faced with a decision, you are afraid to commit."

I looked up at the dark dome and back at Ambrose.

"Kristy, you must understand I am here to help you."
Ambrose came closer and put his hand on my shoulder.

His eyes had a golden sheen. Was that always there?

"It's not that I don't want to know what the key might do.
I'm afraid of what might happen after I use it."

Ambrose sighed and then nodded. "I understand. Why
don't you begin by sitting in the chair? It is quite
comfortable." He took my elbow and guided me onto it.

The chair quietly adjusted to support my hips, back, and
neck. My body melted into the cushions. I have never felt
so light. My eyes were struggling to stay open.

"How does the chair feel?" Ambrose said beaming.

"Like it's part of me." I wiped a drop of drool from the
corner of my mouth. The world seemed to have slowed
down to half speed.

"Good. Let your body relax and empty your mind." His voice sounded far away and his body had taken on a liquid form, shimmering and moving.

I couldn't keep my eyes open any longer and sleep took over.

CHAPTER EIGHTEEN

I woke up to find Ambrose standing in front of me. Feeling slightly disoriented and groggy, I pushed myself up in the chair to get my bearings.

"How long was I asleep?" I asked rubbing my eyes.

"Approximately ten minutes," he said, looking at his gold wristwatch.

I shook my head to clear it. "That's it? It felt like hours."

"Now that you are rested." He pulled his jacket sleeve over the watch. "Have you made a decision?"

I let out a heavy sigh as I leaned back into the chair.

What if nothing happens? Or worse what if something does happen? Will I be the same person? What if I'm so different that I can't live the life I've been living? Then what? Will people recognize me after I leave here?

"I'll use the key," I mumbled.

"Excuse me?" Ambrose leaned closer.

I cleared my throat. "The key. I'll use the key."

"Excellent."

"This is a big step, one you will not regret." He opened his hand toward me.

I took the key from my pocket and looked at it for the last time as I placed it in his palm. He picked it up and read both sides. A radiant glow emerged from his face and his eyes sparkled.

"Fourteen." He sounded pleased. "We have not had this beautiful number in many ages."

"What does it mean?"

"By discovering this key, you have chosen your life path. Fourteen is the path of alchemy. The way of the rainbow." Ambrose raised the key toward the dim light to peer at it again.

"Alchemy? Rainbow?" I shifted in the chair and realized the seat belt was buckled across my lap.

"New beginnings and opportunities await you on this path." He walked to the podium, inserted the key, and turned it slowly.

The room went dark. I looked up as pinpoints of light broke across the sky. There seemed to be millions.

"Wow." More and more stars were being born in the room.

"I must admit, I never tire of this," Ambrose said as he tipped his head skyward.

The chair slowly reclined backwards until I was lying flat. The stars seemed to be moving closer. Or was I moving closer to the stars? I looked over the armrest to see Ambrose and podium far below.

"What the...?"

"Aren't you glad you have the seat belt buckled?" He called out, chuckling.

I grasped the armrest tightly as my body tensed.

What did I just agree to do? This is not what I had in mind.

"I will input fourteen using the key pad. Relax into the chair and open yourself to receive." Ambrose's voice sounded right in my ear although he was far below me.

"Should I keep my eyes open or closed?"

"It will not matter either way. The only things you need to keep open are your mind and heart."

"Is that all?" I whispered to the mesmerizing universe above me.

I took a deep breath and sank deeper into the chair with my eyes closed. A flash of light appeared beyond the cover of my eyelids. It startled me so I quickly opened my eyes. The sky was majestically shining with planets, stars, and galaxies all within my reach. A Milky Way surrounded me. Its vastness was oddly comforting. A galaxy spiraled toward me and I flinched, than realized it was wrapping itself around me. The red glowing cloud moved through and around me. Veins of stardust swirled above my head and below my feet, guiding me to the core of the galaxy.

In the distance, a figure approached. Cassandra's long, sparkling colorful dress shimmered among the stars. Her reddish-blonde curls fanned to the sides as she glided towards me. A long tube made of gold floated beside her. I've never been so happy to see someone as I am right now.

"Hello, Kristy," Cassandra said as she gave me the warmest hug. It was then that I realized I was not in the chair anymore but standing among the stars. She kept me at arm's length after the hug and beamed at me.

Cassandra tapped the gold tube with her fingers and it spun slowly. The number fourteen is engraved on the side of the tube. The latch slowly unhooked and the lid opened. A papyrus floated out and unraveled. Words appeared as stardust floated over it. As if the Universe itself was writing with a calligraphy pen, the words *"Life Purpose"* was scrawled along the top of the papyrus.

"Your purpose in life is to guide and inspire others by teaching the Truth, Kristy. Your intuition is beyond sharp and you are exceptionally courageous," Cassandra said as the page dissolved uncovering a blank one below it.

Another cloud of dust floated over the papyrus. The words "Spiritual Warrior" appeared.

"Spiritual Warrior?" My head felt light and my body vibrated.

"You are a Spiritual Warrior and a powerful being. It's time you fully embraced the talents you agreed upon." Cassandra took a few steps closer to me. "I see the concern on your face. There's nothing to be afraid of, Kristy. You were born for this and you are more than ready."

Cassandra tapped the gold tube once again. "I am also here to warn you about a dark spirited being. She goes by the name of Mara."

The sky opened like a movie screen. The front of the Broken Chalice appeared. People are lining outside the crowded entrance. A woman with long blonde hair forced her way to the front of the line and entered the bar, walking toward the DJ booth. She whispered into DJ Rae's ear.

"Is this Mara? Why does she look familiar to me?" Cassandra nodded and motioned for me to keep watching.

Rae pointed across the crowded dance floor to the bar where Randi and I were serving drinks.

"Whoa. That's me and Randi." I leaned in closer to the "movie."

Mara glided over the dance floor as if parting the Red Sea. She stopped in front of me. My head was down and don't notice her right away.

I remember feeling as if someone was watching me.

Mara took the crystal hanging from her neck and pointed it toward me. A prism of green light shined on top of my head. I see myself look up at her.

"I already know what happens," I explained to Cassandra. "Why do I need to watch this?"

Cassandra raised her hand and continued to watch the open sky.

In the movie, Mara and I ended our conversation, then she turned and walked onto the dance floor. Midway, she looked back toward the bar and a blue beam of light streamed out of the crystal penetrating my forehead.

"That was when I felt lightheaded and went back to the office to lay down."

Sure enough, I say something to Randi and walked up the hallway to the office. Mara emerged from the crowded dance floor and followed me. Dominic, the bouncer, stopped her from going up the hallway. Mara resists but he won't let her pass. She yelled in Dominic's face, pushed aside a few customers and stormed out the front entrance.

The opening in the sky slowly closed and stars reappeared.

"Mara is the dark light, Kristy. She used to be a spirit guide but she decided her own agenda was more important and started using black magic. She would do anything to make sure you don't follow your intuition and share the gifts you were given. Don't let her get to you."

"What does it matter to her if I live my purpose?"

"Mara has a jealous spirit and she tried to prevent you from coming here today. Right?"

My thoughts go back to the woman who stopped me in the Plaza on the way over here.

"That was Mara. Do whatever you can to stay away from her, Kristy."

The gold tube floating next to Cassandra quickly spun around and a golden stream of light emerged from the opening. I watched as the golden light reached out to me, penetrating the center of my chest. A warm sensation filled every cell in my body as I melted into the chair.

Feeling as if someone or something was pulling me back, the golden stream of light flowed out my fingers, toes and the top of my head, retreating back into the gold tube. The lid snapped shut and the tube disappeared behind the dust cloud.

Frantically, I looked to Cassandra for more answers but the galaxy swirled behind her and slowly pulled her in. The vastness of the Universe revealed itself again. Sitting up in the chair, I grabbed the seatbelt to release myself but it wouldn't budge.

"I need to follow Cassandra. I need more information," I said through clenched teeth as I continued to struggle with the seatbelt.

The stars, planets and Milky Way passed me at warp speed and eventually became tiny specks of light. A flash of light appeared and once again the darkness canvassed over me.

CHAPTER NINETEEN

I opened my eyes to see Ambrose exactly where I left him, standing by the podium. The room was dimly lit and the sky was once again speckled with white lights. The key was missing from the podium. He followed my gaze.

"It's no longer of use to you," he said. "You've known all along what your contract involved. This was just a refresher course so you will continue on the path you were meant to follow."

I rubbed my eyes and stretched my arms skyward then unbuckled the seatbelt but remained seated. My brain was trying to process everything that had just happened.

"It can be intense for some people. It is as if someone has reached inside your chest and massaged your soul."

I swung my legs over the edge of the chair and placed my feet on the ground. Pushing myself up, my legs were rubbery and my head was light. I fell back into the chair.

"Take your time," Ambrose said. "Your body needs to get used to gravity again."

"I wasn't in the chair for that long." I waved off his advice.

"Well, it may not have felt like you were gone for very long, but you were actually up for ten hours."

My head jerked back as if I'd been slapped. "Ten hours?"

"Time is different up there." He pointed skyward. "What takes minutes in the universe takes hours here on earth."

"There's still so much I don't understand. So many questions."

Ambrose smiled benignly. "This wasn't meant to give you all the answers. This experience was to reconnect you with your authentic self. The Warrior is who you truly are, Kristy."

I closed my eyes and rubbed my temples. "I don't understand. I'm not a Warrior. I'm just the opposite."

He walked over and put a warm hand on my shoulder. "Let me help you stand."

I pushed myself out of the chair and stood on wobbly legs, leaning against him for support. We made our way back to the first room.

Ambrose motioned me to the couch. "We need to go over a few more things before you leave." He sat across from me and looked me in the eyes.

"It has been a great honor to work with you. Fourteens are my favorite souls and I had forgotten how magical they are to this earth." He paused. "But you must never come back here."

"What do you mean I can't come back? I still have questions." I perched on the edge of the cushion, wide-eyed.

He looked down at the floor.

"That's it? You have nothing else to say?"

Ambrose stood up, clasped his hands and bowed.

"Please, Ambrose. I need more." I looked up at him, grasping at his hand, jacket sleeve, anything to get him to answer me.

He slowly turned on his heels and walked down the hallway. I watched in disbelief as the opening in the wall became solid again.

No explanation as to how I'm supposed to be a Spiritual Warrior? You're not going to show me what I need to do, where to go or who these people are that I'm supposed to inspire. Nothing. Nada. Zip. Just throw me to the wolves. Great. Thanks. For. Nothing.

After a few minutes of staring at the wall, I dragged myself off the couch and slowly made my way down to the entrance. The chill of the night caught me off guard as I pushed open the door. My legs still felt rubbery and my head was unsteady. The crisp, cold air slowly snapped me out of my fogginess and my eyes refocused adjusting to the lamplight.

The Plaza is eerily quiet. Looking into the shop windows, the mannequins appear alive, showing off their extravagant clothing and accessories. My car is still where I left it and the alarm echoes off the adobe storefronts.

"Did all of your dreams come true?" A woman hissed behind me as I reached down to open the driver's side door. My body stiffened at the familiar raspy voice. She leaned her back up against the car, facing me.

"Did he take your vocal cords as payment? He does that sometimes." She chuckle snorted and pulled her coat collar closer to her face.

Cassandra's voice came into my head warning me about Mara. Taking a deep breath, I turned to look at her.

"You don't scare me, Mara." I opened the car door and got in.

Mara crouched down and leaned into the car. "Most fools aren't afraid but soon learn they should be." Her breath is hot on my face and smelled like rancid peanuts. "Watch your step, Kristy, because I will be watching you closely."

"Get out of the way." Mara doesn't budge as I grabbed the door to close it.

"Move," I said loudly through clenched teeth.

"Or what, Kristy? Are you going to use some magic powers the Man gave you? Oh, that's right, you don't have any." Mara threw her head back and cackled.

My face turned hot and anger boiled up in my chest. I kicked Mara as hard as I could and slammed the car door shut. She fell onto her back and her long black coat covered her face. The tires squealed as I drove away. In the rear view mirror, Mara wrestled with her coat and eventually stood up. Her eyes glowed red.

CHAPTER TWENTY

I don't know how long I had been driving through the narrow deserted streets of the city but the rising sun blinded me through my windshield. I had no idea where I was headed, until I saw a sign for Santa Fe Ski ten miles ahead. Climbing the hill, my mind flashed back to the dome room at AIB and everything that Cassandra told me.

This is all so crazy. I'm just an average person, living life like everyone else, day in and day out. It makes no sense to me that I could be some spiritual warrior. This is not something I chose!

I slammed my palms against the steering wheel and gripped it tightly.

I pulled the car over into a vista point and the flowers lining the road seemed to have been splashed with bright yellow and blue paint. The blades of grass were fat and brilliant green, the stones on the walkway gleamed, and the fluffy clouds overhead close enough to touch.

The flowers led me to a narrow footpath. As I walked down it, I felt a subtle vibration beneath my feet, which got stronger with each step. Coming around a bend, a large stone labyrinth appeared and Cassandra was standing in the center. Her eyes were closed and a golden stream of light descended from the sky, entering the top of her head and exiting out her hands and feet. The vibrations below my feet increased as she stood with her arms at her side and her head tilted skyward. I stood in awe as I watched her.

After a few minutes, the golden stream vanished and Cassandra opened her eyes. Looking at me, she smiled.

"I'm so glad you're here," I exclaimed, smiling back at her. "There are still so many questions I have to ask you."

I stepped toward her but stopped in my tracks when she raised her hand. Cassandra slowly made her way back around the labyrinth and took my hand.

"Kristy, you'll always have questions." Cassandra placed her hand on the small of my back. The warmth of her open palm seeped into my skin, and the path of the labyrinth glowed. "Perhaps the labyrinth will help you find some answers."

"How will this help me get answers?" I asked pointing to the stone pattern.

"Ask a question in your mind's eye, and while you are walking the labyrinth, be open to what comes to you. Whether in voices or images, answers will be revealed."

Cassandra placed her other hand on my heart, then walked away.

Any other day, I would've stormed off out of frustration, but after the day I've had what do I have to lose? I lifted my foot with some hesitation and stepped onto the dirt path. My mind wouldn't quiet down enough to think of a specific question.

I wound my way through the maze, my body relaxed and a question became clear. My steps were lighter and my breathing slowed. A cool breeze ruffled my hair. In the distance a hawk cried out, and I thought of Chief.

As I continued around the labyrinth, images flashed behind my eyes like a slideshow. A wide range of emotions flooded my body with each image. A heaviness in my chest, shakiness in my legs, and a fluttering feeling in my stomach were happening all at once.

I felt like I was walking on air as I approached the center of the labyrinth. My mind was clearer and an electricity of excitement coursed through me. All doubts and fears had vanished. I was more certain than ever about what I needed to do. Tilting my face toward the sky, the warmth of the sun sealed the deal.

Jogging to my car, I sped down the hill toward the bar. Screeching into the back parking lot, I barely got it into park before jumping out of the car. I threw open the door and walked down the hallway.

"Hey, Paige," I said as I walked up to a booth alongside the empty dance floor. The front area was now our temporary workspace until the office was renovated.

"What are you doing here so early?" she said abruptly stopping her 10-key dance.

"I couldn't sleep." I tossed my keys on the cluttered table.

"Abigail has been calling and asking everyone if they've seen you."

"Is she here? I have something I want to talk to everybody about."

"No. And she's probably called search and rescue by now."

"Really?" I said, raising my eyebrows. "I haven't been gone that long." A small throaty laugh escaped out of my mouth.

"Apparently long enough for Abigail to be concerned," Paige said going back to her adding machine.

I pulled out my phone and dialed Abigail's number.

"Where are you?" Abigail yelled.

I pulled the phone away from my ear. "I'm at the bar."

"Seriously, where have you been?"

"Are you coming down to the bar soon?" I pushed some papers around, not at all interested in what they said.

"I wasn't planning on it. Why?"

"I need to talk to everybody and it's important that you are here." I sat down across from Paige.

"What time are you doing this?" She sounded annoyed.

"As soon as you can get here."

"I'll be right down." Abigail hung up.

I shoved my phone in my pocket and it clicked against the stone.

"I totally forgot about this." I pulled it out and held it up.

"What did you forget about?" Paige didn't look up but continued punching the keypad.

"The stone."

"I didn't realize you still had it." Her hand stopped mid-calculating.

An image of a jaguar appeared and the hologram showed some kind of medieval knife with gemstones. "Not another one."

Paige peered over at the stone, eyebrows raised.

"Move the stone to see the hologram," I said placing the stone in her palm.

Paige ran her finger over the smooth surface to look at the jaguar. "Is this the first time this has happened?"

Before I had a chance to answer, the back door slammed shut and heavy footsteps echoed down the hallway.

"Okay, I'm here. What did you want to talk about?" Abigail said with her hands on her hips.

"Hi." I shoved the stone back in my pocket and walked over to her, extending my arms toward her. She gave me a light hug and plopped down on a barstool.

"Alight, well I'm going to grab something to drink. Anyone else interested?" Paige shook her head and Abigail stared at the floor.

"This is going to be interesting," I said walking behind the bar.

CHAPTER TWENTY-ONE

Randi emerged from the back storage area as I grabbed a juice from the makeshift cooler.

"Hey, can you join us for a quick meeting?" I gulped down half of the juice.

"Sure," Randi walked around to the other side of the bar.

Abigail was still moping with her elbows on the counter. I motioned over to Paige to join us.

"I've asked you all here because I have some big news." I set the container of juice on the counter and rubbed the back of my neck. "I've decided to travel indefinitely and will give Abigail my share of the business."

A heaviness hung in the air as if the oxygen was being sucked out of the room. The only bright spot was Randi smiling at me.

"You're what?" Abigail said, eyes wide.

"There won't be any money exchanged. I'm simply giving you the business."

"Why are you doing this?" Abigail's voice had gone up in pitch.

"I've realized there are things I need to do and I'm going to start doing them. Now."

"That's great, Kristy," Randi said. "I'm happy for you."

"Thanks, Randi. I appreciate it."

I looked over at Paige. "Paige? You okay?"

"Uh, yeah. I'm just a little...shocked." Paige looked at Abigail. "But if that's what is going to make you happy, I say go for it."

"Thank you, Paige. That means a great deal to me. This is a huge step for even me." I said, placing my hand on my chest.

Abigail crossed her arms across her chest and stared straight ahead.

"Could you guys give us a minute?" I said to Randi and Paige.

"Sure," Randi replied as she and Paige got up and walked outside.

"I know this comes as a shock, but I'm not going to apologize for finally living my life the way it was meant to be lived." I walked around to sit next to Abigail. "You have no idea what I've gone through the last couple of days."

A wave of exhaustion came over me. "It's been a total transformation for me. This thing that I need to do is much bigger than the both of us."

Abigail looked at me as if I'd just told her I'd been abducted by aliens. Which I guessed was sort of true. Except the changes taking place inside me were real. I was learning there's more to life than what I'd been doing. I wanted to make a difference in the world. But I was afraid of failing or not doing enough. How could I explain that to her?

"Abigail," I touched her arm. "I'm actually surprised by your reaction. We've always taken risks in our lives, business and personal. Together and separate. We took a risk with this bar and look how successful it has become. I have no doubt that it will continue to be successful."

"I do want you to be happy." Abigail stood up and stepped toward the dark dance floor. "Are you sure you don't want to think about it longer?" She faced me as tears welled up in her eyes.

"I wasn't expecting this to happen either. I was perfectly happy with my life the way it was until I was shown a different way. I think it's time for me to move on."

"What different way?" Abigail asked.

I felt the stone in my pocket and flashed back to my experience at AIB. "It's one of those things that you wake up one day and you realize there's more to life."

"When will these changes happen? Are you leaving right away?"

"There's still quite a bit that I need to take care of and I want to make sure you're in a good place for me to leave. That for starters." I pointed toward the office that was still a charred mess.

"So are we okay?" I slid off the barstool and walked toward Abigail.

She took my hand. "We'll always be okay, Kristy."

I squeezed her hand in mine.

"So have you heard anything back from the fire inspector?" she said walking to the bar counter.

The timing of her asking that question caught me off guard. *Why was she so concerned about the fire investigation? Is this proof that she had something to do with it? Or is this question coming from a business perspective?*

"Um. No. I guess I can call him."

"Okay. I'll go get Randi and Paige."

"Sounds good." I took my phone out of my pocket. "Hey, Abs."

"Yeah." She turned around.

"Thanks for understanding," I said, smiling.

"Sure." Her smile didn't match what her eyes were saying. *Why am I noticing these little nuisances all of a sudden?* She pulled the door behind her and the click of the door closing echoed through the bar.

CHAPTER TWENTY-TWO

After a long and exhausting few days, my body could barely make it up the stairs to my apartment. When I reached the top I saw Paige crouched on the welcome mat with a brown envelope in her hand.

"Hey Paige. You okay?" I said as I slowly walked up to her.

Paige jerked around and jumped to standing. "I wanted to talk to you about the bar but you left before I had the chance." She held out the envelope to me. "This was on your doorstep."

"I'm pretty tired. Is it serious?" I tucked the envelope under my arm and aimed my key for the door lock.

"I wouldn't bother you if it wasn't."

I pushed the door open to a blast of stale air. The apartment smelled musty. Everything was exactly where I'd left it but I barely recognized the place as mine. I sat on the couch, tossed my keys on the coffee table and leaned back into the cushions. I glanced up at Paige, who stood in the doorway.

She looked over her shoulder into the hallway, then timidly stepped into the apartment and closed the door behind her. She sat on the ottoman by the bookshelf, averting her eyes.

"Are you sure you're okay?" I put my feet up on the coffee table.

Paige was perched on the ottoman sitting on her hands. "I've been anxious since you told us you're leaving the bar to Abigail."

"I trust Abigail will do just fine. Did she say something?"

"No. But…" Watching Paige's eyes dart about the room was unsettling.

"What are you worried about?"

"I know you've been friends for a long time so I'm not sure it's my place to say anything." Paige stood and fidgeted with the ceramic elephant collection on the shelf.

"Paige, you can tell me anything."

She turned around and sat back down on the ottoman. "It's like she has multiple personalities. She's nice one minute and then pissed off the next. I don't know how to handle it. Have you ever experienced that?"

"I've noticed she's been moody lately," I said sitting up on the couch. "I just chalked it up to all the stress with the fire and whatever else goes on in her life."

"I hate to say it, Kristy, but I think she's unstable. Who knows what will happen with the bar when you leave."

"You don't think Abigail will keep the bar?"

"Hard to say because she's so unpredictable." Paige stretched her legs out in front of her. "I guess I feel like you have more common sense when it comes to the business. You leaving scares me."

"I'm sure you're gonna be just fine. Randi will still be there with you and business will continue as usual. It will be like I never left." I smiled at her.

"Do you want something to drink?" I asked turning toward the kitchen.

"Sure." I heard her say behind me.

From the fridge, I grabbed two soda waters. Reaching for the bottle opener on the freezer door, a photo next to it caught my eye.

"Holy shit." I touched the corner of the photo. It's an old picture of me, Paige, and Abigail standing next to Abigail's old Jaguar. The photo was taken shortly after Paige started at the bar. Just today the stone showed me a jaguar and a medieval knife.

"Do you need help?" Paige stood in the doorway looking at me. "Is that us with Abigail's old Jag?" She chuckled as she came up beside me. "I remember that day as if it was yesterday. That car was definitely a lemon."

I took the photo off of the fridge door and leaned up against the counter.

Can I trust Paige enough to tell her about the images on the stone? What if she goes to Abigail with my suspicions?

"Are you okay, Kristy?" Paige said as if talking into a long metal tube.

"This can't be," I said in disbelief.

"What can't be?"

"Remember when the stone showed me the jaguar? Could this be what it was telling me?" I pointed to the car in the photo.

"I remember, but what does it have to do with Abigail's car?"

"If I show you something, do you promise not to tell anyone?" I looked Paige directly in her eyes.

"Yes. Of course."

"I mean it, Paige. No. One."

She nodded her head.

I rushed to the bedroom and grabbed my journal from the bedside table. When I walked back into the kitchen, Paige had a look of bewilderment on her face.

"Look at this." I frantically flipped the journal pages to the middle of the book. "The jaguar wasn't the only image that the stone showed me." I stopped on the page where the dragonfly and police shield were poorly drawn.

"This was the first image." I held the book up for Paige to see. She looked back at me not registering how important it is. I flipped to the second image in hopes a light will go on in her head.

"Here's the second image." I showed her the Zozobra and silver lighter with a "Z" on it. "Can't you see the connection?" My voice is panicky and my heart is racing.

"What connection are you talking about, Kristy? I'm sorry. I don't understand." Paige turned the pages back and forth between drawings.

"There's more." I snatched the journal out of her hands and turned the pages quickly to the Saab logo and bartenders tool. "Just the other day, the stone showed this image and the next day I had a flat tire." I looked up at Paige for validation but all I got was a blank stare.

"Paige, my car is a Saab and the tire was punctured with a bartender's tool. Part of the tool was on the ground," I shrieked.

"It's just a coincidence." Paige waved off the journal and drank from her soda water. "A stone can't cause bad things to happen, Kristy."

"That's what I used to think. But then this last image, the jaguar and knife, makes me believe that the stone has been warning me. Do you know if Abigail has a medieval knife with gem stones?"

She stopped mid swallow, eyes wide.

"Paige?"

"She collects them," she said putting her hand over her mouth.

My stomach tightened and my body felt drained of energy.

It was Abigail after all. The fire, the break-in, the flat tire. But why? Why would she do these things after all these years of being friends and business partners?

I slowly made my way to the dining room table, my legs barely getting me there. Paige doesn't move.

"Do you really think Abigail is capable of doing those things?" Paige spoke softly.

I shrugged my shoulders and covered my face with my hands. "What if it is a coincidence and the images don't mean anything?"

Paige walked over to the table and sat down next to me. "Do you really believe that?"

"There are no coincidences, Kristy." Chief appeared at the end of the table.

I looked at him and then at Paige to see if she heard him. She didn't budge.

"Um. I'll be right back," I said to Paige and motioned for Chief to follow me.

As I closed the bathroom door, Chief was sitting in the bathtub.

"Are you crazy showing up when someone else is here?" I whispered to him pulling the shower curtain wide open.

"Duty calls when duty calls." He shrugged. "This tub is kind of nice." He sat up and stretched out his legs. "Too short though."

"Can we be serious for a minute?" I sat down on the toilet seat.

Chief nodded at me as he fondled the loofah sponge.

"What do you mean there aren't any coincidences?"

"Things that happen in your life and the people you meet are all part of life's plan." Chief squeezed the loofah and a bit of water fell onto his chest. He jumped. "What is this magical ball?" He squeezed it again and more water fell. Chief straightened up and a smile slowly came across his face.

"It's called a loofah. You use it to wash yourself when you take a shower. Can we focus, please?"

Chief reluctantly put the loofah back in the shower rack and turned to look at me.

"I'm here to guide you on your journey. You already know the truth." Chief touched one of the water droplets and stuck out his tongue to taste it.

A knock at the door almost made me fall off the toilet seat.

"Kristy, are you okay in there?" Paige asked from the other side.

"Yeah. I'll be out in a minute," I said turning back to the tub. "Of course."

The tub was empty and the loofah was exactly where Chief had been sitting.

Paige is standing in the kitchen drinking her soda water and looking at the journal.

"Sorry about that," I said leaning up against the counter.

"So what are we going to do with Abigail?" Paige asked as she handed me the journal.

"I don't know. I think I need to catch her in action."

"How are you going to do that?"

"Not sure, Paige. I'll think of something, but right now I'm exhausted. Do you mind if we talk more tomorrow?"

"Oh, sure. I'm sorry for keeping you." Paige finished her drink and put the bottle in the recycle bin.

"Remember, tell no one about the stone and the images. Got it?"

"Yes. Mum's the word." Paige motioned locking her lips and throwing away the key.

I locked the door behind her, turned to walk back to the kitchen and saw the brown envelope on the coffee table.

"You can wait," I said to it as I walked to the bedroom for some much needed sleep.

CHAPTER TWENTY-THREE

The piercing sun through the crack in the curtain woke me up. I rolled over, covering my head with the pillow. Yesterday seemed like a dream. One that gives you a nasty hangover. I dragged myself to the kitchen and made some coffee on autopilot. Grind the beans. Put water in the maker. Pour grounds in the filter. Close cover. Push the start button. An amen seemed appropriate when the coffee machine came alive with its gurgles and drips of liquid black gold. Grabbing a mug from the dish drain, my eye caught the photo of the three of us next to the jag.

"I just need one cup before I deal with you," I said, ignoring the photo.

With coffee in hand, I made my way to the living room and sat on the couch. The hot robust liquid tingled my lips and warmed my insides. I rested the mug on the coffee table and the brown envelope stared up at me.

"Can't a girl catch a break?" I swiped it off the table and held it in my hands.

The only writing on the envelope is my full name. No return address or postage. It's so light that it has to be empty. Opening the metal clasp, I looked inside to find a single piece of paper with a typewritten message. I slid out the note and it read.

It will be mine again
I haven't come this far to
Let it slip through my fingers now.

I looked closer at the text and noticed the 'h' was slightly higher than the other letters and the 'e' was missing the '-'.

This wasn't from a printer. It was typed from an old-style typewriter. I remembered the bookshelf behind Paige's desk at the bar. She loved collecting vintage anything. On one shelf was a small black typewriter she'd found at an antique shop in town. Robert Frost supposedly used it when he stayed in Santa Fe. I threw on some clothes, folded up the piece of paper and walked down to my car.

The hallway to the bar was dimly lit by the red exit signs at each end. It was eerily quiet and the sound of my footsteps bounced off the bare walls. I opened the door and walked over to the bookshelf. The typewriter was right where I remembered. Moving it onto Paige's desk, I found a piece of copy paper in the drawer and fed it around the roller.

My hand shook as I pecked out the word "hello." Turning the knob to raise the paper, the 'h' was level with the other letters.

"Crap." I pounded my fist on the top of the typewriter.

I crumpled the paper, tossed it in the garbage can and placed the typewriter back on the bookshelf in what I hoped was the exact same position.

I need to find that typewriter.

CHAPTER TWENTY-FOUR

Driving past the Plaza, my phone chimed a text from an "Unknown Caller." I pulled over and tapped the green thought bubble.

Roses are red.
Violets are blue.
What you have in your possession
I will pursue.
Be careful where you tread
The who might surprise you.

Who is this? I typed frantically into my phone.

A few minutes passed while my phone sat silent. I dialed my phone company's customer service.

"Thank you for calling Verizon. How may I assist you today?" The friendly customer representative said.

"I just received a text message from an unknown number. Is there any way to find out who owns the phone?"

"Let me look at your account." I heard the keyboard clicking in the background. "Was it the most recent text?"

"Yes. It just came in a few minutes ago." I swiped my finger along the dusty dashboard.

The keyboard clicked again. "It looks like the message came from a pay-as-you-go phone. They are untraceable."

"Damn."

"Is there anything else I can help you with today?"

"No. Thank you."

"Thank you for calling Verizon. Have a good day."

Tightening my hands around the steering wheel, my head quickly searched through my virtual Rolodex as to who would have texted me from a throw away phone.

Is this the work of Abigail? How far would she go? What has happened to my longtime friend?

Pulling away from the curb, I drive aimlessly through the city streets in order to clear my head. After about an hour, I found myself parked outside Paige's house.

CHAPTER TWENTY-FIVE

Her Mustang wasn't in the driveway. I jogged up to her front door and checked it, but it was locked, so I peered in the windows but no sign of Paige. I went through the side gate and tried her back door, but it was locked too. I could see a sandwich with a couple of bites out of it sitting on the kitchen counter.

Did Paige leave in a hurry?

I moved to another window. Cupping my eyes with my hands, I peeked through an opening in the drapes. Scanning the small living room I saw a typewriter sitting on a table next to the couch. *That has to be the one.*

I heard a shuffling noise behind me, and turned to see Chief leaning up against the house with his arms crossed.

"Why must you always sneak up on me?" I whispered.

"It's what guides do." He shrugged his shoulders.

I gave him a dirty look and turned my attention back to the typewriter.

"What are you looking for?" Chief peered over my shoulder.

"Do you see that typewriter?"

"Yes."

"I need to see if it matches a note I received."
"Hmm."

"Hmm, what?" I looked at him with my hands on my hips.

"Why do you think it was Paige who gave you the note?"

"Well, I don't know that it was Paige. I guess Abigail could have used the typewriter without Paige knowing." I peeked in the window. "Maybe they are both in it together."

"Hmm."

Chief was infuriatingly to the point. I rolled my eyes at him. "I also got a text this morning from an untraceable number."

"That's interesting."

"You don't say," I said, but Chief was already gone. "I'll never get used to this," I said again to no one.

A car door slammed out front. I crouched down and could see Paige through a small window in the front door.

She walked into the house and hung the keys on a hook above a table by the door. My eyes had to be deceiving me.

The key chain was a miniature version of a medieval knife about six inches in length, gemstones and all. My heart sank.

No. No. No. No. We trusted each other. I told her all about the images and she told me all about her son. Was that all a ploy to win my trust so she could get the stone? No. I don't believe it. She can't be part of this.

The deadbolt on the back door snapped. Holding my breath, I crouched even lower. The doorknob turned and I prepared myself to make a run for it.

Paige's phone rang and I risked a peek through the window. She had stepped back from the door to answer it.

"Hey," she said. "Are we still on for tonight?"

"I talked to her yesterday."

"Yes. I sent it to her this morning."

"Okay. Sounds good. I'll see you later."

Paige shoved the phone into her pocket and walked toward the backdoor. I saw the knob turn and ran for the gate. Gently closing it behind me I sprinted to my car and drove off.

CHAPTER TWENTY-SIX

I parked around the corner from Paige's house and attempted to catch my breath. Seeing the medieval knife caught me off guard.

Who was she talking to on the phone? Could Paige and Abigail be working together to get the stone? Why didn't they just ask for it instead of being coy?

A loud voice boomed in my ear. I glanced in the rearview mirror to see if someone was in the backseat.

Kristy, you're a warrior, remember? It's time to start acting like it.

I made a U-turn in the middle of the street and drove back to Paige's house. It's time I find out what's going on.

I peered through the window of the front door and knocked loudly; the house was empty.

"Paige?" I called out while knocking hard. I tried the doorknob and it was unlocked. "Hey Paige? Are you here?"

The living room had rustic furniture and antiques were purposefully placed throughout. The typewriter was right in front of me on an old fashioned metal cart. I could type something real quick before Paige even knows I'm here. Taking the piece of paper out of my pocket, my trembling hands fumbled with the typewriter and finally got it on the roller. A noise from the back of the house interrupted my focus and I hurriedly typed "hello" onto the paper. Pulling it free from the typewriter, I shoved the piece of paper in my pocket.

"Paige?" I called out again to make sure she knew I was here.

"I'm back here. Kristy, is that you?" Paige walked up the hallway tucking her shirt into her jeans. "What are you doing here?"

"I...uh...knocked on the door but you didn't answer and the door was unlocked so I came in," I said using my hands to interpret my movements.

"I know we talked yesterday but were we supposed to meet today?" She rolled up her sleeves and straightened her collar.

"No, but I was in the neighborhood and thought I would stop by to ask you something." I jammed my hands into my pants pockets and my shoulders inched up to my ears.

"What about?" Paige raised her eyebrows.

"The stone," I blurted out.

"The stone? What about it?" Paige walked toward the kitchen.

My feet stayed planted to the floor. "Well, um, have you talked to Abigail about it? Told her what it does?"

"You said not to tell anyone. So I didn't." She opened the refrigerator and took out a soda. "You want something to drink?"

"No. I should get going."

"Are you okay? You seem a little on edge," Paige said walking back into the living room.

Do I tell her about the note and the text messages? No. After seeing the keychain and typewriter I'd better keep it to myself.

"Just a little spooked. You know, with the photo of the three of us in front of Abigail's Jaguar."

"Right. That's definitely crazy." She took a sip from the soda can. "Please trust me when I say I didn't say anything to Abigail. I don't fully trust her, especially lately."

"Did something happen?" A chill went up my neck.

"Just what I told you yesterday."

"Maybe I'll call her to see how she's doing." I walked toward the door.

"Ok. Let me know how it goes." Paige closed the door behind me.

CHAPTER TWENTY-SEVEN

On the way to my apartment, I left a message on Abigail's voicemail to call me as soon as she got the message. As soon as I hung up, my phone beeped. Another text from the unknown number.

Meet me at the Plaza bandstand
10:00pm

Who is this? I replied quickly.

Silence.

I won't meet you unless you tell me who you are. I gripped my phone tightly as I angrily tapped the message.

Bring the stone and no one will get hurt

Who is this? I demanded with a reply text.

The phone sat quiet in my hand.

I was too restless and upset to go home, so I stopped at Del Charro for a cocktail and dinner. As I walked into the restaurant, I saw Paige at the bar with a couple of people.

Is this what Paige was talking about on the phone earlier today?

I hurriedly walked past them and into the restaurant.

"Kristy?" Paige called after me.

"Hey Paige. I didn't see you." My face grew hot with the lie.

"Are you meeting someone?"

"Nope. Just me."

"Why don't you join us?" She motioned toward her friends at the bar.

"No thanks. Looks like you're celebrating something and I don't want to intrude."

"Paige!" The woman at the bar exclaimed, turning heads. "Thank you for the flowers you sent." She ran over and gave Paige a hug and a peck on the cheek.

"Happy birthday, Sylvia." Paige smiled. Sylvia trotted back to the bar and promptly drank a shot with the guy in the group.

"I'll let you get back to your party," I said waving off Paige.

"Well, if you change your mind, come on over." Paige made her way back to the rambunctious group and I was taken to a quiet table for one in the dimly lit restaurant.

Dinner was quiet and delicious. When it was done, I reached into my pocket for my wallet and felt a piece of paper at the bottom.

Pulling both out at the same time, I realized the paper was from the typewriter at Paige's house. I had totally forgotten to check it. My heart raced as I laid the piece of paper on the table, ironing it flat with my hands.

The lighting wasn't very good so I had to use the flashlight from my phone to see the word clearly. Moving closer to the paper, I saw the word "hello." The "h" was higher than the other letters and the "e" was missing its dash.

I almost fell out of my chair.

What now? Do I confront Paige and tell her about the note and that it came from her typewriter? What about the keychain?

I needed some air. I left money for the bill and walked out to the front. Paige and her group were no longer at the bar. Frantically, I scanned the restaurant in case they decided to have dinner. No Paige. I rushed out the door and looked up and down the street only to find it empty and dark.

CHAPTER TWENTY-EIGHT

The Plaza wasn't far from the bar but I didn't feel like walking the few blocks this late at night. I pulled up to the curb just around the corner from the bandstand. People were hanging outside the Underground while drumbeats escaped the front door. My heart was racing and I knew I needed to calm down, to prepare myself for whatever was about to happen. I tilted my head back onto the headrest, closed my eyes, and took deep breaths. I felt the stone in my pants pocket, and took it out, hoping to see an image on it, some kind of message or clue. It was blank. I shoved the stone back in my pocket and looked at the clock on the dash.

9:45

As I walked up the street toward the Plaza, I thought I heard my name called out behind me. I turned around, but no one was there. Rounding the corner by the Orr House, I heard my name again, louder and closer. I didn't turn around because now I was sure it was just my imagination. I pulled my jacket closer around me as I crossed San Francisco to the small park in the middle of the square.

The Plaza was deserted. The only light came from the black lampposts framing the park, and I could still hear the pounding of the bass from the Underground. The breeze pushed dry leaves around the empty streets and tree branches waved at me.

Suddenly someone jumped on my back and hugged my neck with their arms. I felt myself falling backwards but somehow the rush of adrenaline kept me upright.

"What the…" I yelled as I grabbed the person's arms.

Paige jumped off and landed in front of me with a huge smile on her face.

"Paige, what are you doing here?" I said in my strictest parent voice.

"I could ask you the same question." She danced around me.

"No, really. It's late. Are you here with your birthday friends?" I looked behind us to see if they were waiting for Paige.

"We went to the Underground to dance. You should come." She grabbed my hand and attempted to pull me toward the club.

"I can't, Paige. I'm meeting..." I trailed off.

"Who are you meeting? Hmmm?" She raised her eyes brows and her voice was almost teenaged.

"Nobody." I let go of her hand and walked away from the bandstand. I didn't want her to know my final destination.

There was a slight breeze with a bite. I shoved my hands into my pockets for warmth. I was again reminded of the typewriter results and pulled the piece of paper out of my pocket.

I had to ask Paige if she wrote the note. What did I have to lose at this point?

"Hey Paige, you remember the envelope that was on my doorstep that day?" I said turning around to face her.

"Uh. Yeah."

"It was a hand typed letter with few sentences basically saying that "it will be mine" and "I won't let it slip through my fingers now.""

"What does that mean?" She scrunched up her face.

"I can only guess that it's about the stone. But the interesting thing was the "h" and "e" was slightly off. The "h" was higher than the other letters and the "e" was missing its dash. So it was typed on an old style typewriter."

"That *is* weird. Why would someone send you a typed letter about the stone?" She stopped underneath a street lamp.

"I don't know. When I was over at your house the other day, I tested the typewriter you had in the living room to see if it was the one that was used."

Paige stepped back.

"And it typed exactly like the note did," I said handing her the piece of paper with the word "hello" typed on it.

Paige leaned in toward the lamp to get a better look at the paper. "Oh my gosh, Kristy." She looked up at me with wide eyes. "You're not thinking I did this, are you?" Her hand flew to her chest.

"I honestly don't know what to think, Paige. Who else has access to your typewriter?"

She looked up at the sky and ran her fingers through her hair. Her head snapped down to my eye level and her eyes lit up.

"Abigail. She asked to use my typewriter right after the fire. I didn't think anything of it." Paige covered her mouth with her hand. "Is that who you're meeting tonight?"

"I'm not sure. They didn't say who they were in the texts."

"Texts? It wasn't just the letter? Where are you supposed to meet?" Paige looked frantically around the Plaza.

"You should leave, Paige. I don't want you involved or to get hurt." I started walking toward the bandstand.

"You're not getting rid of me that fast." Paige walked up next to me and wrapped her arm around mine. "I'll protect you." She smiled and giggled.

I stopped in my tracks and looked at her. "This is serious, Paige. Who knows who this person is and if they are violent."

"Well, if it's Abigail, we have nothing to worry about. Why would she hurt either of us over a stone?"

A scuffling of feet by the bandstand stairs interrupted our conversation. Paige took my arm again and a chill went up the back of my neck. I let out the breath I didn't realize I'd been holding.

We slowly walked toward the noise and a dark figure stepped out of the shadows. The light from the lampposts illuminated their face. Paige gasped and put a tighter grip on my arm.

"Abigail," I whispered into the cold, dark night.

She stopped mid-stride. I motioned Paige to stay put and I stepped closer to Abigail.

"Don't get any ideas," I said placing my hands in front of me.

"What are you talking about?" Abigail glanced at Paige and then back at me.

"Aren't you the one that sent me the note and texts to meet here tonight?"

"No. I got a text to meet here. They sounded like they were from you." Abigail's voice was shrill. "Then who sent us the messages?"

My vision narrowed and my heart raced.

Why are the three of us here if Abigail and Paige weren't the ones wanting the stone?

A person emerged from the back of the bandstand and came up behind Abigail.

I knew those glowing red eyes and black cloak.

"Mara." Her name rose up from the back of my throat.

"It's so nice to see you and your friends, Kristy." Mara spread out her arms as if to embrace us.

Paige gasped and Abigail stepped next to me.

"Who are you?" Abigail demanded.

"Just a friend. Right, Kristy?" Mara moved toward the three of us.

"What do you want, Mara?" I said with clenched teeth.

Mara pulled her black leather gloves onto her hands tighter and a demonic cackle escaped her throat.

"Oh, Kristy. You act so tough but then again you are a warrior." Her fingers made air quotes.

I clenched my fists and my body stiffened in preparation to fight off Mara.

"No need to get all tense. You can make this very simple. Just give me the stone and I'll be on my way." Mara reached out her gloved hand.

"So it *is* the stone you want."

"It's rightfully mine. You see, Kristy, I've had that stone for centuries before you found it. As I'm sure one of your guides shared with you, I was once like them. Guiding you mere mortals through life's journey when you were too weak to carry on. You were all so high maintenance," Mara hissed, pulling the cloak collar closer to her face.

Abigail touched my arm. "What are guides?"

I waved her off as I stared down Mara.

"Anyway, I decided to go out on my own and the Counsel wasn't happy. So I was disbarred and became just like you." Her crooked finger pointed jaggedly at me.

"You are nothing like me. Us." I looked at Paige and Abigail.

"That's true. I actually have powers." Mara's right hand flipped upward.

My legs collapsed underneath me and I fell to my knees.

"Kristy," Paige gasped and rushed to my side.

"You can do whatever you want to me, Mara, but leave these two out of it." I struggled to stand with Paige's help.

"Just give me the stone and no one will get hurt." Mara held out her hand.

I took the stone from my pocket and held it tightly in my hand. I slowly opened my hand, revealing the blank stone.

Something came over Mara as soon as she saw it. It was as if she was looking at a long lost child. A yellow glow emerged from the stone and pulsated to the beat of a heart. Mara rushed toward me with both hands in front of her.

"Not so fast." I snapped my hand shut right before she reached me.

Mara stopped abruptly staring at me with her red beady eyes. Her nostrils flared and a growl surfaced from her clenched jaw. Paige and Abigail stepped closer to me and I motioned to them to back off.

"Before I give you the stone, I need to know one thing," I said crossing my arms.

"Were you the one that made those images appear on the stone?"

Mara stood tall, with shoulders back and a gleam in her eye. "Why yes, it was I."

"And you were framing Abigail and Paige in hopes I would turn on them?" My heart raced and heat flushed through my body as the anger welled up inside me.

"Wasn't that brilliant?" Mara tilted her head and let out a guttural laugh.

"If only it had worked." I held the stone in between my fingers.

Mara's laugh stopped short and she peered at the stone. She was mesmerized by it. She reached out to take the stone from my hand.

"No," Paige yelled lunging forward at Mara with the medieval dagger in her hand. Mara quickly grabbed Paige's hand and turned the dagger toward her.

"Paige, no." I grabbed her by the waist to stop her.

She stiffened and went limp. We both fell to the ground with Paige falling on top of me.

"Paige?" I slid her off. She stared up at me. "Can you hear me?" I brushed hair off of her forehead. "Please say something."

Wet sounds came from her mouth. My hand scanned her chest and stomach for blood. Her jacket was sticky and wet.

"You're going to be okay." I applied pressure on the stab wound and looked for Abigail. She and Mara were both gone.

Paige grabbed my arm and looked me in the eyes as she tried to speak. I leaned in closer.

"Go make the world a better place," Paige barely whispered.

Abigail came running from behind us. "I lost her, Kristy. I'm sorry," she said trying to catch her breath.

"Stay with me, Paige." Tears burned my eyes. Abigail held Paige's hand and sobbed.

The stone lay next to her on the sidewalk.

CHAPTER TWENTY-NINE

Leaving the cemetery after Paige's funeral, Abigail and I drove up to the trailhead in Jemez Springs. To think it had only been a year ago that Abigail and I did our annual hike. The crisp air filled my lungs as we walked up to the ledge overlooking the valley below. The stone had been blank since that night in the Plaza and Mara hadn't reappeared. A few feet off the trail a ponderosa towered over us. I squatted down at the base of the tree and dug a deep hole with my hands.

"Back to where you belong," I said to the stone, placed it in the ground and covered it with dirt and ponderosa needles.

Abigail and I decided to sell the Broken Chalice to business partners from Southern California. Hopefully, the bar will continue being successful with Randi as the manager. As for me, it's time to move on and make the world a better place for Paige.

As we walked back down the trail to the parking lot, I heard a rustling sound behind me. I turned to see Chief, Cassandra, and Doc following me. It was comforting to know they'd be with me in this next chapter of my life.

ACKNOWLEDGEMENTS

I am forever grateful to my sister, Chris Imbasciani, for her unending support and tough love. This book wouldn't have been completed without her.

Thank you to my editor, Jordan Rosenfeld, whose honesty and insight made this book brighter.

Thank you to all of my friends and family who put up with me for the last six years and the look I gave them every time they asked how my book was coming along.

We are all Warriors.